ALSO BY MICHAEL SYMMONS ROBERTS

Soft Keys
Raising Sparks
Burning Babylon
Corpus

MICHAEL SYMMONS ROBERTS

Patrick's Alphabet

VINTAGE BOOKS
London

Published by Vintage 2007

2 4 6 8 10 9 7 5 3 1

First published in Great Britain in 2006 by
Jonathan Cape
Random House, 20 Vauxhall Bridge Road,
London SW1V 2SA

www.vintage-books.co.uk

Addresses for companies within The Random House Group Limited
can be found at: www.randomhouse.co.uk/offices.htm

The Random House Group Limited Reg. No. 954009

A CIP catalogue record for this book
is available from the British Library

ISBN 9780099483786

Mixed Sources
Product group from well-managed
forests and other controlled sources
www.fsc.org Cert no. TT-COC-2139
© 1996 Forest Stewardship Council

Printed and bound in Great Britain by
Bookmarque Ltd, Croydon, Surrey

FOR ROBIN ROBERTSON

PATRICK'S ALPHABET

I

A was written in blood where the bodies were found. It was paint, but the story went round town that it was blood. More than that, the story said Michelle had dipped a finger in her gaping chest, to write a message on the concrete car-park wall. She had finished the first letter, then collapsed.

The first letter of what? Her friends said it must have been the name of the killer. She was writing ADAM SLIGO, but her life ran out at A. Her sister Ally clung to the idea that it was ALLY I LOVE YOU, or ALLY DON'T WORRY. There was even a stupid theory that it wasn't A at all, that she was desperate and unable to shout, that she struggled to the wall and tried to write HELP in her own blood. It was really H, but she was so weak that the uprights fell into an A.

A few people knew that it was paint, and knew it had nothing to do with Michelle. The police who were second on the scene were certain she had never left the car. The shots were fired at close range through the windscreen of Jake's old blue BMW. Jake and Michelle both died in their seats. All the blood, and both victims, stayed inside the car.

I had evidence that Michelle didn't write the A. I got there first as always. I had to get my work done before it was all cleared up. When I arrived, they were both dead, and in the background of my shots the wall is clean.

Proof counts for nothing unless it's your own proof. I've thought a lot about this. I could have had one of my pictures blown up to billboard size and stuck it on the town hall. The red paint could have been sent for analysis, and the results bellowed through a megaphone by a man in a white coat. It wouldn't change a thing for those who thought Michelle had left a final, cryptic message.

Far from fading, as the weeks passed, the story grew. A lot of people in this town needed some last word from her. So I kept quiet about what I knew.

And what I knew at the start of that summer was this: after the murder, someone took a can of red paint and daubed a letter A at the crime scene. From the look of it, they used a brush and took some time. It was not a message. End of story.

It's a map-maker's term. I like to say I live on the edge of the edgelands. My flat turns its back on all the houses. My windows gaze across car-crushers, gasometers, hypermarkets, sewage works – a mile-long no man's land between streets and fields.

I can't work out how there was a fatal smash out there. My best guess is joyriders up from London for the night, looking for a racetrack with no speed cameras.

I make good time, since all the roads are clear. On these summer evenings, the empty business parks return to plan – a grid of tarmac strips, right-angle turns, green mounded roundabouts. But between the new buildings old wilderness is flourishing: scrub woodlands, towering grasses, brick wreckage of factories, workshops, homes. The police channel's on as I drive, and their nearest car is still five miles back. This is easy.

I think of Fellig – the master – the only ambulance-chaser in New York to have a police radio fitted in his own car. What am I talking about? The only one ever. The ambulances had to chase him. He got to the smashes, fires, murders, so fast they'd barely happened. That's why the girls on the radio called him Weegee. He was so quick he must have been getting tip-offs from the dead.

But I'm quick too. Especially on my home turf. M4 corridor, M25 west side, suburbs and dormitory towns; I know every inch. Unless you die in bed, the chances are I'll take the last shots of you.

The edgelands are at their best tonight. The late sun picks out warehouses and offices – two breeds of building, one all metal, hunched and sealed; one all glass, evolved to live on light. I turn left past Collegiate Insurance, but on the hinge of the turn the sun hits the mirrored face of the Collegiate Tower like a colossal flashgun. Everything goes black, then through purple and magenta. In the seconds it takes to slow down and get my vision back, I hit something.

My eyes clear and I see a big dog slouching away. Its coat is flashing in the sun, prismatic, almost dazzling. But its coat is outshone by its amber eyes. It breaks into a run, and slips between two buildings.

My little accident has brought me within a car's length of the old BMW. It's in the middle of a big concrete courtyard walled on three sides by metal-shuttered warehouses. A dead end. I steer around the car and circle it once. There's no one around. No other car, and the body of this one is rusty but intact. It doesn't look like a crash. Only the windscreen is shattered, and I can make out two figures slumped in the front seats.

I park about twenty feet from the BMW and get out. Time is tight. That patrol car can't be too far away now. I pull the camera out of its bag and take a wide shot. Head on, car with smashed windscreen. No bodies, just a good general shot to sell to any paper. Then I move in for the details.

Close-ups are harder to sell, but people want to see them. If they're strong, there's a market, if not in the press then on websites. I can see the driver is a male, slumped forwards like he's taking a nap at the wheel. The passenger is a girl, and she's fallen back and sideways onto him. There's a lot of blood. The engine is ticking over. That's strange, the old engine idling, as if they just pulled in to look at a map.

I'm still taking pictures, but I'm weighing it up. I was expecting a car smash, but this is more like a Mafia hit. What comes to mind is those Sicilian pictures of a crusading mayor ambushed on his way to work, caught as he stumbled from the car, upper body in a dark pool on the road, feet still tangled in the pedals.

The boy has been shot through the neck, once at least. She's taken it in the chest, her face is blue-white except for a trace of blood around her lips. Maybe they tried to knock the gunman down? Or hand-brake-turn the car and leave him standing? They must have tried something, since the engine is still running, but it hadn't worked.

I'm remembering the first book of photographs I ever saw. It was called *The Rock 'n' Roll Generation* – American kids in diners, at the drive-in, on the open road. There was one shot – through a windscreen – which was just like this scene. It showed a couple, parked up, and it looked like they were making up after a row. The guy was leaning forward on the wheel, obviously upset. The girl had her head on his shoulder, trying to explain it to him. Whatever it was.

It must be said, in photographic terms, this couple I'm framing make a fine picture. The dead do give great photographs. Pictures of the living look like frozen glimpses. Somehow, you feel you're not getting the full scene. The dead are different. Their silence fills the space inside a frame. These two were a picture waiting to be taken. As I take them, I can feel their shape – solid and exact – adding to the weight of the camera in my hand.

Imagine saying this to a child: 'Doubt everything they tell you.' Whoever *they* are. When I found a fossil snail in the quarry, I put it in my grandmother's hands. I was guessing at hundreds of millions of years. So many hundreds of millions that stone had swallowed all the animals.

Her hands were like gloves – loose and clumsy. She turned the fossil snail and then said, 'It's a fake.' I told

5

her I had cracked it from the rock myself. She handed it back to me, snail down, and went back to her pots of jam.

I'd like to think she was a literal believer in a seven-day creation. I'd like to say she sat me down with the Book of Genesis and argued that God had laid the fossil record in the rocks to cover his creative tracks, or to give his children a sense of history. I'd like that, because then I could dismiss it.

In fact, there was no Bible in the house. No books at all. She didn't trust them. She believed nothing and no one. 'How do you know,' she asked one morning over breakfast, 'that I'm not poisoning you?'

So, years later, when the police came to my door, wanting to comb my photographs for evidence, I said, 'How do you know I haven't doctored them?'

They can invent what they want. I'm not giving up my chemicals. Four baths. Developer first, the real magic. It still feels like I'm conjuring the images from nothing, out of blank sheets.

I get home and take the film from the camera. Night is cooling so I close the windows, open the curtains. I look out across the edgelands and see blue lights heading for the warehouse yard, pointless sirens howling in the empty roads. I step into my darkroom and begin my alchemy.

I drop a clean sheet in the first tray. Darkness bleeds into it, greys and blacks in the shape of a car. I work through the images – developing, stopping, fixing, washing – then I peg them to the drying racks.

They are great pictures, but when I get to the close-ups of the girl I can't look. She upsets me. Maybe it's something about her face, but I've seen the faces of a thousand corpses. Whatever it is, it's physical. My guts make a fist and my heart jitters. I pull her out of the developer, and don't know what to do next. I can't bring myself to throw her pictures out, so I peg them up without putting them through the stop bath. That seems right somehow. Without the acid to arrest it, her image will bleed darker and darker until all the paper is black.

Usually by this stage I'd be on the phone to the picture desks, but this time I just leave the prints pegged out and walk around the flat turning off all the radios.

I'm not thinking straight, and I've forgotten to clear up the darkroom. As I go back in I knock my thermometer off the wall. It breaks in half as it lands in the basin. Its silver spine smashes into beads like shot. I've never had to handle mercury, but I know it isn't good for you. I swill it down the sink, nudging it along with the side of my hand. Then I wipe my hand and worry that maybe I shouldn't have touched it at all.

It's not a good night. I feel I've lost some bearings. I sit in silence in a chair by the window. That bay window was the reason I chose this flat decades back. I was looking for a modern place – low maintenance – but when I saw the old convent split into apartments, and this second-floor flat with all its glass facing out across the edgelands, I knew I had to have it. Some of the plaster's flaking off the walls now, a fine white dust on the dark stained floorboards, but the view is as good as it was the day I moved in. The edgelands are dark and still tonight. I can see across them as my eyes adjust, even out beyond them into fields of grain and rape. In the middle of this prairie, I make out the distant wall of poplars which boxes in a tiny farmhouse, protecting it from gales, and from the vanishing horizons of its crops.

The doorbell. It's very late. No one calls here except by arrangement, to pick up photos. There's no arrangement for tonight. I open the door on a chain, and see a young man dressed in blue overalls, head shaved.

'I've moved in down the corridor. You probably saw the van last week. Wanted to introduce myself.'

I switch on the light and let him in.

'Saving electricity?'

'No,' I say, 'I just like it sometimes.'

'Great place. You been here long?'

'Long time, yes.'

'I like the high ceilings.'

We stand in silence. He isn't leaving. He has a soft, clear voice, the kind I like to hear. But I don't like making conversation.

'Do you want a cup of tea or something?'

'No need,' he says, and eases a bottle of whisky from the lining of his coat and a glass from each side pocket, setting them down on my table.

'I'm afraid I don't really drink spirits.'

'Not at all? Or not with strangers?'

'Well, no . . .'

'How about neighbours? I'm sure you'll help a neighbour celebrate his new home.'

So we have a drink, and he talks about his move.

He says he's a rep for a publishing company, this is his new patch.

'What kind of books?' I ask.

'They call it "Mind Body Spirit".'

'Right.'

I can't think of anything else to say. He breaks the silence.

'What do you do?'

'Photographer.'

'Weddings and stuff?'

'Not really.'

He gets up and strolls into the darkroom. He's seen the pictures pegged out through the open door. I go after him.

'Please don't touch anything.'

He stares at my M4 shots from the previous day and winces.

'You work for a paper?'

'Lots of papers.'

'Specialise in accidents?'

'General freelance, but a lot of accidents and crime . . .'

'You make a living out of this?' He turns to look at me.

I say, 'I've got low overheads.'

'I wasn't talking money,' he says.

I walk back into the front room and he follows me. He doesn't notice the shots of the murder scene going black on the line. I've got one picture framed on my living-room wall. He stands in front of it.

'One of yours?' he asks.

'Course not. Don't you know it?'

'It's horrible,' he says. 'What happened to her?'

I explain that she's married now, with kids. She lives in Canada, I think. I tell him she's met the photographer since, even met the guy who dropped the napalm.

'Napalm?' He looks astonished. 'Who is she? Where was this?'

I want to say, 'You should know this. It's the most famous picture in the world.'

'Vietnam war,' I say instead.

'Why is it on your wall?' he asks. 'Were you there?'

'No, it's just an amazing image.'

He looks at me for a long time.

'It's a child in agony,' he says finally.

'She's fine now.'

I tell him how Weegee once took a shot of a mother and daughter crying as they watched their tenement burn down, with two other daughters trapped inside. The New York fire regs were changed within a week. But he's never heard of Weegee. He keeps staring at the Vietnam shot.

'I wouldn't have it on my wall,' he says.

I want him to leave, but he reaches for the bottle to pour himself another drink.

'I've got an early start tomorrow, so I'll need to get to bed.' It's about as subtle as I can muster.

He stops, looks down at his feet in silence for a moment, then looks up at me.

'Forgive me, it's none of my business,' he says. 'Did I upset you?'

I tell him it's fine. There's nothing to forgive.

'We never did names,' he says. 'I'm Martyn, with a

10

"y". Martyn Calladine. Does the name Calladine mean anything to you?'

I shake my head.

'My uncle was a famous American preacher and healer.'

I don't know what to say.

'And you?' he says.

'I'm Perry.' He reaches across, and we shake hands. He smiles, pours a couple of drinks and hands me one.

'There's a lot to tell about my uncle.' He walks across to the window and takes a swig from his glass. 'A great man. A great man indeed.'

In the midwest of America in the early 1970s, a healer and his entourage rolled up in a small farm town and raised a tent. On the first night he only got a few punters. He took away a woman's back pain and a man's stammer. Then the local drunk stood up and started giving him abuse. The healer stepped down off the stage and walked to the back of the tent. He stood face to face with the drunk until the drunk stopped ranting. Then the healer told him his life – straight through – youngest son, born with a withered leg, mocked at school, despised by his father, left school, couldn't hold down a job, got the girl next door pregnant, married her, hit the bottle, beat her up, the whole saga.

By the end of it, the drunk had gone from rage, through astonishment and embarrassment, and now he was sobbing like a baby. The healer knelt in front of him and put his hands around the guy's bad leg. Nobody had touched that leg since he was a child, and he'd have pulled a gun on anyone who tried, but this was different.

The healer held the leg, quite tightly, closed his eyes and said, 'In the name of the Lord Jesus, be whole again.' Then he got up off his knees and tapped the drunk on his forehead, just dabbed him with a finger. The drunk hit the deck, he was out cold for a few seconds. When he got up, his crippled leg was as straight and strong as the other one.

He was stone sober, and he walked out of the tent with his mouth hanging open. As he got into the night air, he realised he could run, so he ran and ran for sheer joy, ran all night. The story goes that he heard crickets all around him as he left the tent, crickets and cicadas making music with their legs, an orchestra of leaping things celebrating his miracle, and that's what set him running.

Anyway, he got back with his wife and son, fixed himself some work in the construction business – hard physical work, so he could use his leg – and he became a member of the local Baptist church. He wasn't devout, but he showed up most Sundays with the family.

A couple of years later, his construction firm was taken over by a big concern in Illinois and he moved away. No one in his home town heard from him again.

About five years later, that same healer was on tour again. It was his last tour, as it turned out, but he didn't know that. By then he was billing himself more as an evangelist than a healer. He still healed, but some charlatans had given healing a bad name. In a couple of cases, the newspapers had uncovered utter cons – athletes paid to leap out of wheelchairs, throw away crutches. But this healer really did heal.

So he was between cities, waiting in an airport lounge to get to his next gig, when he heard a rumpus at the bar. Some guy must have touched up the barmaid, because she was screaming, and the guy was holding his hands up trying to pretend nothing happened.

The healer recognised him instantly, even after all those years. He remembered that this was the drunk from the midwest. So he walked up and confronted him.

'Can you still walk?'

The drunk looked quizzical.

'I said can you still walk?'

The drunk came out with a stream of abuse.

'So is this how you repay the Lord, when he makes you whole again?'

The guy was so drunk he couldn't focus on the healer, and the barmaid was still screaming. The healer left him. Prayed for him, then left him. What else could he do? The man got a miracle, got the one thing he ever wanted, and still he turned his back on God.

I like the story, and Calladine tells it well, but I have a question.

'Is it true?'

Calladine looks baffled.

'Course it's true, Perry. I don't tell the other sort.'

'So what does it mean?'

He can see I'm fascinated. He sips his whisky and grins at me like he's just pulled off a trick.

13

II

I'm driving back from the motorway. It's lunchtime.
I'm keen to get home to develop my shots, and to
eat. Then I see it from the car and I slow down. I
don't connect it with the A at that moment, but it
does strike me as odd. I'm wondering if it's something
to do with the murders. Everyone in town thinks
Adam Sligo was the killer, and he's still on the loose,
so it crosses my mind this might be his game.

I stop to take a picture. As I'm framing the shot, I
see Petra Ware coming towards me. She's coming out
of the edgelands, back towards town. I guess she's been
to see the place where her son was killed. It's become
a spontaneous shrine, so many flowers and soft toys
and cards that the camping shop in town has put an
awning over it, to keep the pilgrims dry.

I hear she goes there every day, and spends the rest
of the time just walking. No one knows if she's looking
for the killer, or if she's just deranged with grief. She
doesn't talk.

With this in mind I take my picture quickly, and
turn to head back to my car.

'Wait,' she calls. 'I need a word with you.'

I don't want to wait, but she knows I've heard her.
She hasn't said a word to me since we left school, and
she didn't say much to me then.

I say, 'Sorry about your son, Petra.'

She nods. 'There's a rumour you've got pictures of the murder.'

'I've destroyed the film. Don't worry, you won't see anything in the papers.'

She seems oblivious to my answer.

'Did they say anything to you?'

'No,' I tell her. 'It was over by the time I got there. I didn't know he was your son.'

She keeps staring at me, as if she doesn't believe me, as if she's trying to force me to come out with it. I point at the B to explain what I'm doing, but she isn't interested.

In the car, I'm thinking about the B. It could have been coincidence, but it's the same red paint, and even neater than the A. I try to rationalise it as a game – Adam Sligo's game – so if the A was at the murder scene, the location of the B should be significant too. It's on a bus shelter, daubed across a poster of a woman running through the white surf on a beach. I think it's a perfume ad.

I get back to the flat to find a letter on my doormat; a note from Martyn Calladine inviting me to his place, so he can return my hospitality. It's for dinner tonight. That gives me a few hours to come up with a reason not to go.

They say that by the time the police arrived at Petra Ware's front door, she knew her son was dead. The night of the murder was Michelle's birthday. Her friends had planned a party, and Jake was in on it. Jake was to pick her up from work in his car, then bring her to the Huntsman bar where they would surprise her.

When Jake and Michelle failed to show after an hour, some of their friends walked round to Mrs Ware's to see if there had been a mix-up. On the way, they saw the blue lights flashing past, heading for the edgelands. As soon as she saw who was at the door, she collapsed, blacked out on her own front step. When she came round, she said, 'Jake's gone. There, I've said it.' She had felt anxious for weeks, had sensed that some disaster was looming. The previous night she'd had a dream about her house, but the house was empty, no furniture, no family, just bare boards and walls, and the wind screaming through the glassless windows.

So it was that the moment Jake's friends turned up to find him, long after he was due at the party, she knew. She knew there and then, and there was nothing his friends could say to talk her out of it.

The young policewoman sent to break the news found Petra in a trance, not interested in the news she had come to break. Within minutes of the WPC leaving, Jake's friends were naming Adam Sligo. His red pickup truck was seen heading for the edgelands earlier in the evening. TJ had seen him, because TJ lived just across the road from Sligo. It must have been him. TJ knew Sligo kept guns, and if anyone was enough of a psycho to use them on Jake and Michelle, it was Adam Sligo. TJ kept guns too, but he was the real thing – trained ex-regular army. He didn't like it when civilians started playing soldiers.

Word got around very quickly. Jake and Michelle were

dead. Sligo was armed and missing. Within an hour, TJ and his brothers were on the roof of Sligo's bungalow. They had air rifles tucked under their arms, and stretched out between them was a huge banner saying LYNCH THE BASTARD. Down below, the rest of the kids were shouting support from the front lawn. Petra Ware got to hear about this and rushed down to stop them. She pleaded with them to let the police handle it, but in her heart she must have wanted Sligo dead.

Of course, neither he nor his pickup came back to the house, but those kids stayed on the roof for hours. Even if Sligo was missing, they could still terrorise his old man. After all, he'd raised a killer. Petra didn't like that. She peered in through the net curtains, expecting to see Sligo's father cowering in a corner. Instead, she could just make out in the failing light a hunched and static figure in a chair, oblivious to everything, blankly watching TV with the volume on full. After seeing that, Petra started walking. She walked out to the edge-lands to see where her son had died, then she walked back, and she's kept on walking, twelve to fifteen hours a day they say, in and out of the edgelands.

No luck thinking up an excuse for Martyn Calladine. Not a solid one anyway. He seems the type who would only accept a solid one, and besides, it might be good to have a bit of company for an evening in these strange times.

'Did you work out what the story means?' is the first thing he says when I walk in. I must be looking blank because he says, 'My uncle's story . . .'

I shrug, like I don't care what it means. I'm annoyed with him for playing games. I'm thinking about going for a snoop around his flat, like he did in mine, but I notice there's another man sitting in the corner of the room. He's quivering as if he has some current running through him.

'This is Maurice,' says Martyn. I nod.

With what seems to be a great effort, through chattering teeth, Maurice issues the words 'NAME . . . IS . . .' then grins and sobs at the same time.

'Come on Maurice, tell my neighbour your story.' Martyn's grinning too.

To my surprise, because he doesn't seem capable of telling a story, Maurice produces a string of words, chosen for economy. Each word is more than measured, it's relished, as if he has just invented the rudiments of a language and we are his first pupils.

'THIS . . . IS . . . MAURICE . . . VOICE.' I turn to Martyn, and ask 'Do you look after him?'

'He doesn't need looking after. It's just a case of getting used to it.'

'Used to what?'

'Speech. The power of speech.'

'Are you some kind of therapist then?'

'Look,' snaps Martyn, 'how blind are you?'

'What?'

'VOICE,' said Maurice.

To my mind, the healer – Calladine's Uncle Jim – told that story first as a warning, a warning to honour the proofs you see, because you won't see too many.

You don't get many chances to take the right path.

Trouble was, I couldn't be sure what I'd seen that night. Maybe I did see a dumb man speak. If he was deaf and dumb from birth, then it's no wonder he was struggling for words. He was new to the whole game. Then again, he could have faked it. Maybe he'd been talking all his life.

III

For three days after the murders Adam Sligo didn't stray more than a couple of hundred yards from the scene of his crime.

Once he'd emptied his gun into Jake and Michelle, he drove around the corner, past the warehouses, and disappeared into the Bluebird Centre, still open for late-night shopping. According to the newspapers, he spent the first few nights in there.

The rest of the story I got first-hand. Mister Motor is his trading name, a friend of mine. His business is in the edgelands, about half a mile from the Bluebird Centre. He divides his time between clamping and crushing. His teams tow the clamped cars back to Mister Motor's yard, and he waits in his office, behind a metal grille. He does shifts, alternating with his son. You can't blame him for sharing the burden. Everyone who visits him is livid, baying for blood.

So he's on duty one afternoon and a man arrives in a pickup truck. He parks and walks into the office. He looks like a commando, full camouflage gear. But his voice is quiet, and he isn't angry. He says he wants to buy a car.

Mister Motor clamps and crushes, but he doesn't sell. The commando says he doesn't want a car to drive, in fact he doesn't need an engine. He wants the shell of a car, and in particular he wants the shell of a blue car. Mister Motor tells him again that he doesn't sell, and he sends the man on his way.

Mister Motor doesn't see him for an hour or so, then, just as he's locking up the gates to go home, he hears the sound of breaking glass from the corner of his yard. Furious, he storms over there to see what's going on. But there's no sign of anyone. That's worrying. Anything could happen in that yard, with wrecked cars piled up ten-high boot to bonnet. The last thing he wants is kids climbing around.

Mister M calls, but no reply. He shouts and shouts, but no reply. He hears a sound, like a coughing or choking, and shouts again, but no reply. Much against his better judgement, but with no other options, he climbs into the piles of wrecks to see if he can find the intruder.

It's a difficult climb, into and out of broken, smashed-up cars – in through the rear window, back seat, front seat, out through the windscreen. He's getting sliced and stabbed by the broken glass and metal. Finally he finds the commando sitting in the driving seat of a written-off blue family saloon. His head is slumped over the wheel and Mister M fears the worst, but when he reaches him the man is sobbing. His face is smeared with blood from the cuts on his hands.

Mister M starts to give him some grief, but the man splutters something about his mum. This was his mum's car, he says. So Mister M – still fuming – tells him even if it was his mum's, it isn't now, because every car in the yard is waiting to be squashed into a tin can. And besides, he says, this idiot is risking both their lives and breaking the law by being here.

The commando isn't making much sense, says he wants to buy the blue car. Mister M has lost his rag by now, screams out the facts again – the blue car's in a pile of cars ten-deep and isn't up for sale. He threatens to call the police if this lunatic doesn't get out of the car, and out of the yard, right now. The man doesn't move, and Mister M climbs out towards his office to ring 999.

I was still a boy, about nine or ten, when I was sent to stay with my grandmother while my parents were splitting up. Of course, they didn't say that. They said they needed to redecorate the house, but I never saw the house again. Nor my father.

Anyway, I was staying in the countryside, and I hated it. I hated my grandmother and her old, cold house. So one night I ran away. I took no food or drink and had no plan or route in mind. I only lasted one night.

When it was time to sleep that evening, I went into a copse at the side of the field, looking for a bush or something to hide under, and in the middle of the copse I found a car. It was an Austin Cambridge. A real car abandoned in the woods. The trees and bushes had grown around it, adopted it as one of their own. So it was almost completely camouflaged. The doors were rusted shut, but there was no windscreen, so I climbed in through the front. Once I'd jumped across into the back seat, I was in another world, a world of warm, dry leather, leaves and catkins. I felt completely safe, and I've never slept a better night than that. Ever since, I've felt that cars were on my side.

Years later, I heard that Weegee made his car into a home. He furnished it with developing kit, spare flashbulbs, cameras, typewriter, clothes, salami and cigars. That Chevy coupé was his bedroom, office, diner, darkroom.

So when I heard that Sligo ended up crying in the front seat of a car like his mum's, I felt quite close to him. Perhaps it was his mum's car? The papers would have looked into all that, if they'd known why he was in the car. But Mister Motor kept that to himself, and me.

By the time the police arrived at the yard and Mister Motor pointed them towards the blue car's shell, Sligo was gone. He'd been dripping blood all the way through the yard, but the drips stopped at the road outside. That's the story.

It's the day after Sligo was seen in Mister Motor's yard and I'm in town. The place is crawling with hacks and photographers. I don't like so many cameras in one place, so I'm trying to keep a low profile.

I'm there because the police have announced they're making a statement about Jake and Michelle's murder. I go along to hear the statement, but I'm also thinking I'll get a few shots of the press corps. No mileage for me in taking pictures of the police like everybody else, but maybe I could sell a shot of the press crowding in on this poor little town.

I'm surprised to find I feel ashamed of my hometown. I know every square foot of the place, and I've photographed most of it too. As small market towns

24

go, it's not a bad one. There's still plenty of old red brick in the centre, clustering round the market square, and the town-hall clock still means something to locals like me who grew up setting our watches by its chimes.

But there's no market nowadays, not to speak of, just a few stalls of cheap trinkets. No chimes either. The clock's been mute for years. And there's more and more concrete creeping in alongside the brick. Concrete and franchises – burger bars, coffee shops – the same as every other old market town. I know what they're thinking, these press boys from the city. They're wondering who on earth would live in a rundown two-bit town like this. It's written all over their faces.

They take up positions on the pavement outside the police station. The cops come out, and start to say their piece, and a man in the middle of the press pack tries to interrupt them. He shouts so loud that one of the police says, 'We'll be taking questions later.' But the man keeps shouting, 'I've got something important to say,' and by this time the journalists around him are getting wound up, trying to stop him. He's ranting, and as the crowd shifts I catch a glimpse and see it's Maurice. I'm amazed. His speech has come on so fast. He could hardly get a word out a few days ago, and now he's gabbling.

'Listen to me! If you don't purge this town of evil, we, the people, will do it ourselves!'

It's heading for a fight or an arrest, but just as it looks like kicking off, Maurice turns and barges his way through the press corps. The police carry on with their spiel. He brushes past me, catches my eye, but I look away and hope he doesn't recognise me. When he gets to the back of the crowd he keeps walking, and a dog follows him. It's the same dog I hit with the car in the edgelands, same eyes, same flashing coat. It walks to heel as if Maurice is its master, then he turns a corner and the dog keeps going. Must be a stray.

I turn back to the press conference. The police chief says forensic evidence proves Adam Sligo killed Jake and Michelle. They've found the gun that fired the shots, and his prints are all over it. They've found his pickup truck too. All they haven't found is Adam Sligo. The policeman bats away a few questions, then it's over. The hacks disperse to speak their stories into mobiles. Photographers race off to get their pictures on the wire.

I have nowhere to rush to, so as they're leaving I notice we've been standing on a red stripe, a curve. It looks like a mark for some new streetlight or a drain, but it's brushed not sprayed. And I recognise the colour.

I don't know why, but I'd assumed that the scarlet-painted A and B would be the end of Sligo's lettering. I was wrong about that.

It takes me a couple of days to track Petra Ware down again. She's always walking, which makes her difficult to trace. I find her at the end of an afternoon of solid rain. Driving back from a job, I see her coming out of Sligo's bungalow. My first thought is that she's killed the old man. All that walking, grieving, brooding, and no explanation. Sligo is still on the loose. No trial, no examination of motive, no remorse. The old boy is the only contact she has left with the man who killed her son. He is the only way of hitting back.

I offer her a lift, make some weak joke about the monsoon, and she climbs in beside me.

'Isn't that Sligo's house?'

'He hasn't a clue who I am, you know.'

Afraid of the silence, I ask a few guarded questions and she tells me she's been shopping for the old man twice a week. She brings him food, cooks him a meal, discusses what's on TV. He never offers to pay, never thanks her for the food, but that makes it easier for her. If he knew who she was, if there was some emotional transaction between them, she would find it unbearable.

Despite TJ and his brothers climbing on the old man's roof, despite visits from the police and door-stepping reporters, he never mentions his son, and seems to know nothing at all about the murder. Petra has, she says, been making these visits from the week after it happened.

'Why do you do it for him?'

'It's not for him.'

By now we're on the outskirts of town, heading for the edgelands. She sits forward in her seat, as if trying to read a distant road sign, then asks me to stop the car. She wants to get out. I tell her she'll be drenched, but she insists.

I pull up outside the Multiplex. There are teenagers – mostly around Jake's age – standing in the entrance, waiting for one film or another to begin. I wonder if Jake used to come here, and if that's why she wants to stop. There's a row of light-boxes by the swing doors, each with a posed still from a film in it. One's called *The Distance*, and the picture is of a man running across a desert. He looks like he could run around the world and not be out of breath. More to the point, he looks exactly the way I'd imagined the healed drunk in Calladine's story. Exactly. The same lank, centre-parted black hair, denim shirt and jeans, boots that look too heavy to carry in a run. It's as though they took the picture from inside my head and used it to advertise a film. It's a strange feeling, like being robbed and chosen at the same time. The man in my head is running across lush, cicada-filled grassland, not sand. I like my picture better.

She's about to shut the car door – without thanking me for the lift – when I reach across and hold it open.

'You asked me if Jake had said anything.'

'You said no.'

'I shouldn't have.'

'What did he say?'

'She.'

'What did she say?'

It's all too fragile. They found that out. Our lives are – my life was – built on nothing. Their deaths were built on nothing. I wanted to tell her to stop trying to understand what happened to her son. It was without meaning. A motive from the killer may have meant something. Locking up Sligo, or lynching him, may have meant something. But she didn't have any of that, so she wanted some message from beyond the grave. I gave her one.

28

I saw it as an act of pure mercy. She didn't want to know that when I reached the BMW they had both already crossed into silence. It didn't matter what the message was, as long as it was unclear. I couldn't risk inventing a simple one, not knowing the details of their lives, their relationships. So I chose a single word and put it on the lips of Michelle. I gave her the word SHANTY, and Petra took it in. For a moment, she looked quizzical, but not disappointed. I shrugged my shoulders and she set off in the pouring rain to turn it in her mind. At last she had a message, and the message was the meaning. She had something to work on — *Shanty. Shanty. Shanty. Shanty . . .*

IV

As the days passed, and there was no sign of Sligo, the newspapers began to drop us. There was a spate of spin-off stories about mad, insular market towns and debates about gun laws, then they left us to it. I kept up my old contacts for crash and crime of course, but I gave them nothing about the double murder. Michelle's close-ups had turned black on my drying racks. The shots of Jake and of the pair of them I kept, but hid them well.

In that first week, the hacks had scrambled to outdo each other. One stranger struck up conversation in the Huntsman bar. He said he was a businessman, just asking out of interest. But there was something about his questions. Too much detail. He made the mistake of asking TJ and a bunch of Jake's other mates.

'Isn't this where her party was going to be?'

'D'you reckon it's true that Jake and Michelle had an argument that night?'

'I read somewhere that she was pregnant . . .'

They took him round the back behind the bar, where the old beer crates were stacked up. His business didn't bring him here again.

In that same week, one of my contacts – a cub reporter on the *Evening Post* called Alex – came to my flat. He asked if I had any shots of the M4 smash that morning; capsized lorry, long queues, driver with a broken bone or two. It was not the sort of thing they usually took from me, so I hadn't bothered to print them up. Alex was offering good money, said they were running a piece because the queues were so bad. I said I would get him a few shots, but I didn't want him in my darkroom, so I left him in my window chair, staring out over the edgelands. I worked fast, and that took him by surprise. When I came out of the darkroom he leapt. He was sifting through the piles of prints I keep on my dining table. I told him he was wasting his time. He came clean straight away.

'Come on Perry, you were there.'

'I didn't take any.'

'None at all? Come on!'

'Well, I didn't develop them.'

'Why are you hiding them?'

'I said I didn't print them up.'

'Look, it'll be your biggest payday. Everyone wants the crime-scene shots on this one.'

He could tell he was getting nowhere, but he couldn't work out why. Nor could I. He had an answer to every reason I gave him not to sell the shots. And he was right every time. Yes, I've sold countless crime scenes. Yes, I could use the money. No, I didn't know Jake and Michelle. I fobbed him off with one wide shot of the car. No bodies. I didn't want to give him any more.

He got angry, threatened to boycott all my work, to ring his friends on other papers. If he went back to his editor without the shots of Jake and Michelle he'd be sacked. If his career went down because of

32

me, he'd take me with him. For once I was relieved when the doorbell rang. I was even pleased to see Martyn Calladine standing there. He said he'd heard shouting, came to see if I was okay. I told him. Calladine walked over and put a hand on Alex's shoulder.

'You don't have to be like this.'

Alex shrugged away and started bad-mouthing me. Calladine stared at him, muttering very fast under his breath. At first I thought it was some kind of spell, then it just sounded like gibberish. Alex tried to ignore it, but Calladine was moving slowly closer and closer to him. The dance continued until Alex had his back against my table. Calladine kept inching forward, chanting louder and faster. Alex arched backwards over the table and Calladine leaned with him so their lips were brushing. Now he was almost singing the gibberish, spitting it right into Alex's face.

Alex collapsed backwards onto the table, spilling my prints all over the floor. He squirmed sideways out from under Calladine, running for the door. Calladine slumped to his knees, then rolled over onto his back, still chanting, but quietly again, almost under his breath. He lay on a gloss carpet of overturned coaches, crushed sports cars, multi-vehicle pile-ups and a lorry dying in its own spilt pool of molasses. He had his eyes closed. Apart from his lips, he was completely still.

There is something else, and it's starting to bother me. It's a good two weeks since Sligo was last seen and I'm out early in the morning. No tip-offs on the police channel, but there is a thick early mist sitting low on all the roads. My nose tells me it's worth heading for the motorway before the morning rush.

Weegee worked on nose too. That police radio in his car was a mixed blessing. It's become an explanation – so *that's* how he did it. Not so. He got to some of those crimes before the killer turned up, before the killer knew he was going to be a killer. If he'd been more of a showman, he could have done *before* and *after* shots – *Pool Hall with Players / Pool Hall with Corpses*. To be as good as that takes instinct.

I'm good too. I'm cruising in the fog, with the camera bag riding shotgun beside me. I head out through the edgelands, and as I reach the Collegiate Tower I slow down and glance at the murder scene. In the early morning haze the cream-coloured awning stands in the mist like a temple. All around the edge, and tied to the sides and roof, are flowers – all colours – each bunch a personal response to what happened there. Yet the whole scene looks dressed, co-ordinated. Under the awning is the gold flutter of night lights and in the middle I can see Petra Ware. I want to stop and take a picture – not to sell, but for the sheer strange beauty of it. I don't, because I can't face her again, so I drive on.

A few hundred yards down the road a dog steps out in front of me. It doesn't run, just steps out and stands in the middle of the road as I steer round it. It's the same dog I hit on the day of the murder – a weird-looking animal. Could be a stray, or a lost farm dog. I pull in to the kerb. My palms are sweating, my head's a pulse. Maybe it was the near miss with the dog, but it wasn't that near. Maybe it was seeing Petra at the shrine to her son. Whatever it was, I've lost the will to go out working. I put the camera bag down in the footwell, and rest my head on the wheel like Jake. Calm down. Like Jake without Michelle on his shoulder. Calm down, calm down. I close my eyes. All I can see is the glow from the shrine, the night lights turning the cream canvas awning into a lantern.

There must be dozens of flames there, hundreds of tiny flickering candles. Yes, candles. Like the candles at the murder scene. No, not like them at all. They were wrist-thick, slow burn, heavy-duty candles, fifteen or twenty of them, all around the courtyard where the old BMW was shot up. I told no one about the candles. They were not there when I first arrived, when the bodies were still in situ. They appeared, like the letter A, hours later when the police had cleared the scene, when I went back to see if there was anything worth shooting, when I photographed the A. I shot the candles too, then I stamped them all out.

For the sake of privacy let's call him 'Z' and her 'E'. When I say they were old I mean hunched and tired, arthritic and forgetful. But they had always been good people. All their married lives they had longed for children, but it never happened. They assumed that God must have his reasons, so they accepted it. Anyway, one night they were getting ready for bed and Z went for a wander in his garden. It was summer, and he liked to end his day this way. He was pinching off dead rose heads, tapping his wind chimes with a finger, when a voice came into his head. It was a voice he'd heard before, not like his own thoughts, or a memory, but something separate. He'd heard it before, only at times of great crisis, or temptation, or doubt. It had come at turning points and helped him to take the right road. He knew it was the voice of God. As it spoke his name, on this hot night in his beautiful garden, he thought it was going to call him home.

'Come, tired servant, your work is done.'

But instead, it seemed to say, it did say . . .

'You're going to be a father.'

Words failed him. Thoughts failed him. It was a bleak joke, after all those years of longing. But the voice went on.

'Your son will be a great man.'

Z knew this was the same voice he'd heard before, but he also knew that his wife would be struggling to make her gnarled joints carry her to bed, and he knew that the voice should have called them to the next life, not given them a new life to care for in this one.

'This can't be right,' he said aloud. 'We're almost dead!'

But the voice snapped back.

'Since you have not trusted my voice, I'll take yours away until the baby comes.'

Z went to bed in silence, and slept badly. In the morning, when his wife spoke to him, he could only make shapes with his lips. He was dumbstruck, as a punishment for doubt.

'Was that another one of your uncle's miracles?'

'No, no, no,' says Martyn Calladine, but he doesn't

36

say whose it was. He is staring at Maurice across a square baize table. It's rather faded. A card table, I guess, a folding one. I notice it because it's one of the few objects in Calladine's flat. In the middle of the green table is a bottle of whisky and three glasses. He pours three large shots. His story is a good one, but I think it's meant for Maurice.

'Okay, okay. I know you're right,' says Maurice finally.

'Good man.' Martyn raises a glass, and we both raise ours.

'Do you want to come to a party?' Now Calladine turns to me. Maurice grins.

'What? Now?'

'Next week, probably Wednesday night.'

'*Probably* Wednesday?'

'Okay, definitely. Will you do us a favour?'

I don't want to get involved. I can't imagine what kind of party he would hold. Seeing how he scared the reporter out of my flat rattled me. But when he invited me for a drink at his place I half-hoped, half-feared that I'd hear some more of that wild gibberish, or at least he'd explain what he did to Alex. In fact, he doesn't mention it at all.

His flat. I know he's pretty new around here, but it looks as though he hasn't unpacked at all. In fact, it wouldn't take him long. There are no boxes or tea chests, just a couple of suitcases. Apart from the card table and a few folding chairs, the flat's bare. All the walls are bare too, apart from one picture over the fireplace. It's an old framed poster of the Marlboro man, a cowboy with a cigarette on his lip, gazing out across the prairie. I nearly spit out my whisky when I see it. He gave me such a browbeating about the picture on my wall.

I say, 'How many kids were lured into smoking by that poster?' He looks up.

'And did you know that cowboy actually died of lung cancer, the model in the poster?'

Calladine says nothing.

'Is that something you should have on your wall?' I'm enjoying myself now, sensing a weakness, buoyed up by the whisky. He stares at the picture for a long time. Maurice looks at me and raises an eyebrow. Calladine stands, lifts the picture off its hook, and throws it face down to the floor. The glass shatters. He pulls out the poster and tears it up. Then he comes back to the table.

'Good call,' he says. 'It's not mine. Comes with the flat, but I shouldn't have left it up there.'

He fills his glass again, and Maurice's. I put a hand across the top of mine. He reaches into a pocket and pulls out a soft-pack of cigarettes. He offers them, and we both shake our heads. We wait for the laugh but it doesn't come. He lights his, takes a deep drag. I notice it's filterless.

I've spent a lifetime washing my hands. Washing off the chemicals. Washing off the germs. As a boy, I needed reminding of the importance of this, and my grandmother did that job. She did it every day, every mealtime, every time I came in from outside. Now it's deep inside me; the rubbing, the wringing and the rinsing. I don't need reminding any more.

It's the dead of night and I've woken with the feeling that my hands need washing. The tap runs and runs. My hands turn automatically like fat fish playing in the water. Only this is serious. I have to get it off, but I can't remember what *it* is. It could be the mercury from my smashed thermometer a few weeks back. I'm still a little worried about that. Or it could be the developer from Maurice's portrait, the favour Calladine asked of me. By this evening there were dozens of posters up around town with my picture of Maurice and a headline MY LIFE CHANGED, SO CAN YOURS, plus the time and venue of a meeting on Wednesday. I hope nobody guesses I took the photo. They didn't tell me it was for a poster. I would have complained, but the D took my mind off it. It took my mind off every-thing actually. There it was – in scarlet – on the white of my car. On my own car. Maybe that's it. That's what I need to wash off – the smell of paint and turpen-tine. It must come off, even if I have to rub my hands to the bone.

V

All week I've been catching sight of him and Maurice outside shops, in and out of pubs, standing at traffic lights talking to drivers. They are giving out flysheets for their meeting, inviting people to come.

It's late afternoon and I'm on my way back from the motorway. Martyn Calladine stops me at the lights around the corner from my flat.

'Well, well, well,' he says, handing me a leaflet.

'Okay, I'll be there.'

'I know you will,' he says. I'm nodding, but I don't know what he thinks I'm coming for. I'll be there, out of curiosity alone, and with my camera ready.

'It's time we did something about this town.' He looks like he means it, and I wonder who he means by 'we'.

The lights are still on red, and I'm lost for words. I notice that dog, the dog that keeps running out in front of me. Calladine sees me looking at it.

'I've got a follower,' he says. 'I'm calling him Paddy.'

'Paddy?'

'You ever read *Patrick's Confession*?'

'Patrick who?'

The lights have changed and the driver behind me is losing patience.

'Just Patrick . . .' His voice tails off. Cars are pulling out and moving past me. Horns are blasting, but somehow I can't go until he lets me. He keeps staring, cool as cool, oblivious to all the noise.

'You should read it,' he says.

'Is this some sort of game?' The moment I say it, I can see it's hit him hard. He looks crestfallen.

'A game?'

'Telling stories . . .'

'The lights have changed, Perry.' It's a while since he's used my name. It makes me feel better and worse. He leaves me and walks towards the car behind, leaning down to talk to the driver who is blasting his horn at me. As I slip the handbrake, Paddy sniffs at the wheel of my car, then at the door, where I scrubbed off that letter D. He can probably smell traces of turps.

Watching the dog brings back a memory. I'm not sure if I trust it, but the memory says a dog saved me one night, the night I ran away from my grandmother's house, the night I found a beautiful car to sleep in. I think it saved me from the cold. In my memory it was an arthritic collie, like my grandmother's dog. I woke in the night freezing cold and the dog climbed gently into the car, curling up next to me on the back seat, keeping me warm.

It can't be true. My grandmother's dog was so crippled it couldn't walk from the house to my hiding place, let alone jump up into a car. But now the dog is so firmly tied to the memory of that night, I can't have one without the other.

I can't decide if I've been targeted or blessed. Either way, I've been singled out. Maybe Sligo knows I'm documenting the alphabet as he writes it, and he's making my job simpler by putting the D on my car. Perhaps I have been marked. Perhaps I'm next on the hit list. Adam has no reason to dislike me. I don't know him as such, though we were on nodding terms before the killings.

Then again, I can't help wondering if Sligo can stay alive much longer in this town. There are so many people looking out for him, and he was bleeding so much all those days back in Mister Motor's yard.

I never remember dreams, but that night I was on a riverboat in Africa, an elegant, old-fashioned steamer. I was old-fashioned too. I was wearing a white suit, sitting on the deck drinking tea. We pulled into a clearing in the dense forest, and along with my fellow passengers – all looking like extras from *Death in Venice* – I stepped ashore. We were in a village, but the local people were taking no notice of us. They were caught up in their own drama, and we stood aside and watched.

Men and women, looking sombre, some even crying, formed a long line from the heart of the village to the riverbank. There were no children anywhere to be seen. I didn't notice where it came from, but suddenly the top of the line was moving, as a bundle was passed from person to person. It was about the size of a cat, wrapped in leaves and tied with crimson sashes. As it passed down the line, everyone kissed it, muttered something, then handed it on. We stood and gaped in silence. A couple of my fellow passengers got cameras out — big Weegee-style boxes — and started to frame up. I was seized by an impulse to join the ceremony, but the villagers were standing so close together that the only free space was at the end. I moved into position, standing with the shallows of the river lapping at my shoes. It was very vivid. I remember looking down at those shoes in the water — lovely chestnut brogues — then along to see the passing and the kissing.

Before I could prepare myself the bundle arrived, dropped into my arms by the weeping woman next to me. Suddenly, I could see why she was crying. In a circle of leaves was the face of a baby girl. Eyes closed. Dead. I didn't know whether to gag or cry. I did neither. I kissed her face, it tasted of salt and stone, sea and river. I looked up the line of people watching me, and I knew what I had to do. I knelt in the shallows and floated her off down the river. She had no basket, not like Moses, and no hope of rescue. She simply floated off, returned to the water.

I woke up with the horrible feeling I'd been shouting, or crying, in my sleep. The dream remained vivid. I tried to rationalise it. My grandmother told me to unpick dreams, not to look for meanings in them. The funeral — well — there was plenty of death on my mind. Why Africa though? I've never been. But at the same moment I thought about that line of villagers I remembered their name. Ashanti. They are the Ashanti people, and my mind is playing word games. They might have been singing sailors, or Hindu mystics, but they were an African nation instead. No

meanings, just word games. My own invention –
Shanty – was coming back to haunt me.

Why did he disguise the names? I still don't get it.
Zecharia and Elizabeth, it's there in the Bible. 'Z' and
'E', he was talking about them as if he knew them,
as if I might meet them, and he felt duty bound not
to break their confidence. It took me weeks – and I
do mean weeks – to work out why Calladine told
that story. I had to understand it, so I could be strong.
He was starting to suck people in, and I wasn't going
to be one of them.

Here's the message. Old Zecharia wasn't struck
dumb as a punishment. It was a gift of grace. Most of
the time, we're left to our own devices, to get through
as well as we can, using our best guesses. Clear signs
are few and far between, so if you get a shot at certainty
for once, well, you've been blessed.

The guy in Calladine's uncle's story – the drunk at
the bar, the guy whose leg got healed – he just got
the one chance, and he blew it.

By that time, I'd had two. Hearing Maurice get
his voice back was one. Losing my stomach for the
motorways was another. Calladine was telling me
not to resist. Read the signs, or face the conse-
quences.

But it sent me the other way instead. As soon as
someone says, 'Trust me', let alone 'Follow me', I'm
out the door.

*

45

I sold them the picture. Perhaps that was a mistake. I don't know. I don't know how to judge these things any more. If I hadn't sold them mine, they could have got it somewhere else.

As soon as I heard, I went down with the camera. I knew the papers would want it. A couple of women – one of them Petra Ware – stood under the awning. A few night lights still glowed. It was more shocking in the flesh than I'd imagined – a gash of red paint cutting across the awning's honey skin. I photographed it on a long lens, so as not to disturb the mourners. Then I went home to print it up and call the picture desks.

It was in the papers the next day, with words they don't often use, like 'desecrate', and 'sacrilege'. While the town was still raw with grief, someone had shown contempt for their feelings. Someone had insulted them all – the living and the dead, victims and mourners. One paper even suggested that the murder scene had been used by drug dealers, and the painted letter E could be a sign of what they were selling.

Alex called that night.

'What's up with your neighbour?'

'Nothing.'

'You're joking! He should be in hospital. A special one. Secure, you know?'

'Did you ring to talk about Martyn?'

'Oh, it's Martyn is it? Martyn what?'

'Goodbye, Alex.'

'Wait. I called to do you a favour.'

With mock concern, he warned me that the town was turning to me for an explanation of the desecration. The story was going round that I'd been seen graffitising the awning, then photographing it, to generate some income. People were outraged. Reporters on the streets were picking up threats against me. I'd better be careful. Rumour was that they were getting together a lynch mob. I thanked him and put the phone down. Then I locked the door and drew all the curtains.

It was the colour of cream on the back of a spoon, the colour of ivory piano keys. It was open-topped, white-wall tyred, super-charged. Each one, before it was sold, was tested at a ton on the racetrack. If it passed, it could go on sale, with a brass plaque on the dashboard stating the exact three-figure speed it had achieved. The Auburn 851 was always my dream car.

Tonight I'm hiding in my bedroom, like the old days. At my grandmother's house I would lie on my bed and stare at my poster of the Auburn. I reach up on top of my wardrobe, take down the poster and unroll it. I stick it to the bedroom wall to see if it still works.

A 1933 Auburn parked beside a Sunderland Flying Boat at Calshot Spit. I didn't know, I don't know, where Calshot Spit is or was. All that matters is that the road ends there, and sea begins. A couple – elegant in long coats – and two Pekinese dogs are leaving the car and walking towards the plane. The dogs are tied to the lady's wrist. Where are they going? Out. Away. Oblivion. I have memorised every detail – the four great blurred propellers and curtained portholes of the

Flying Boat, the stars and stripes above its nose hanging lank against a breathless blue sky. But most of all I have memorised the car; its mirror-polished chrome, the gentle tilt of its windshield, the driver's door ajar, inviting me to step into all that dark tan leather, to step on the gas and go. I tape the poster to the wall, sit on the edge of my bed, and stare for what feels like an hour. Then I take it down, roll it up, and put it back on top of the wardrobe.

All night, if I have a soulmate in my isolation, it's Adam Sligo. When I cover my ears against the shouts from the street below my window, he's next to me, crouching with his fingers in his ears. When the phone keeps ringing, he understands why I can neither answer it, nor unplug it. And in the early hours of the morning, when half a brick shatters my window, I can feel his fear. He's shaking alongside me as I pick up every jigsaw piece of glass and wrap them in a newspaper. It's us against the town, against the world. We are the lonely. We are the scapegoats.

I sit in my overcoat for the rest of the night, shivering by the absent window. When the sun spreads out across the edgelands, I call Alex's mobile, wake him up, and tell him everything. I tell him all about the A, B, C, D and E, about the candles at the crime scene, and the fact that I've recorded it all, not done it, but documented it. I give him chapter and verse, and offer him pictures of all the painted letters. But I don't offer him the shots of Jake and Michelle.

I stay one more day in hiding before Alex's paper comes out and gets me off the hook. He calls round to get the pictures at lunchtime. He doesn't stay long.

I board up my broken window and spend the day listening to the police channels, knowing that I can't leave the building. By the end of the day, I know I've been duped. There were no baying crowds on the street outside, just one smashed window. Alex got his own back, and got his story too. I'm feeling less sorry for Sligo now, more for myself. After all, Sligo's a killer.

VI

Suddenly, the town is full of hacks again. Alex has given me money not to talk to other newspapers, but they are all cooking up their own stories anyway. The details, and especially the photographs, have opened up a whole new line of rumour and speculation. Candles at the murder scene, painted letters appearing across town; what seemed like a one-off act of madness starts to look more like a ritual.

Although I'm hunting for letters now, I'm still trying to pan for gold on the motorways too. I've blown any chance – as if I ever had one – of a Weegee-style hotline in my car to help me with the job. The police never liked me anyway, but now I'm shooting murders and mysterious letters as well as crashes, they like me even less.

How much less, I find out in the early hours one Sunday morning. Their call-out just said it was an Audi capsized on the grass bank at the roadside, but I have a hunch there's more to it. When I get there – first as usual – I realise I'm right. Staggering along the road – too drunk to walk, let alone drive – is a junior Home Office minister. Not too junior either, he has started to appear at press conferences deputising for his boss, and he's spearheading the government's tightening of the gun laws in the wake of the shooting of Jake and Michelle.

It is too good to be true. I can write my own cheque for these shots. He tries to bat me away, then tries to hide his face behind his hands, but he's drunk and slow. I get him in close-up, wide-shot with the car behind him, everything.

I do the job, then pack up and leave. As I'm pulling out onto the quiet motorway, I see the blue lights flashing in my rear-view mirror. My timing, as ever, is spot on. I don't give them another thought as I head for home. I'm thinking of my camera, like a safe or a treasure box. I'm guessing how much money is locked inside it, wound tight into the one film, the ten or eleven shots. Six months' salary? A year's?

The sun is just beginning to show as I drive back through the edgelands. Even the gasometers look beautiful, monumental, in such dramatic light. I put the radio on, and for the first time in a long while I tune away from the police channel. I find some music, some strange Chinese strings, and let it play me home as it drifts in and out of focus, disappearing into white noise, then sharpening again.

I swing into the driveway to the flats and see a police car parked outside. If I'd seen it a moment sooner, I would have swept past and made myself scarce. Too late. I've been seen. I get out, they get out. I know them by sight. They are the pair who were sent to the murder scene.

I try to walk past, but they stop and invite themselves in. One asks me why I didn't give them the pictures of the candles and the alphabet, before I gave them to the papers.

'You must have seen it all,' I say. 'Everything I shot was there for anyone to see.'

While I'm talking to one of them, his colleague opens the back of my camera – my treasure house – and pulls out the film so the morning sun can flood it.

Softly, softly, almost too slowly to perceive, my childhood is coming back to me. Detail by detail. Picture by picture. I'll be in the darkroom with my chemicals, and the taste of a berry or the cold touch of a dog's nose will come back to me from nowhere, and with it more of my story.

Tonight it's a phrase that comes back, a fragment of speech. I'm pouring myself some coffee before going to bed, and the words float into my head.

'You are a liar.'

It's my grandmother's voice, and it's steady and sure.

'You are a liar.'

But I didn't think I was. Not deliberately anyway. I had been climbing the oak tree in the back garden, and I'd overreached myself. I was, literally, out on a limb with no idea how to get back and down. I couldn't call her, because I couldn't face the lecture. That was if she came to help, but somewhere in my bones I knew she wouldn't come even if she heard me call. So I held on for a while, then tried to get back along the bough. I was halfway along when a small branch came away in my hand and I fell.

'You are a liar.' Like a tape-loop, like hypnosis, everything I said after I came round met with the same reply.

Admittedly, it was strange that I woke with a

headache, curled up in an Austin Cambridge, woken by her old dog that came out looking for me. I'd been out all night, but the why and how were a mystery to me. I had no memory of the time between my fall from the tree, and coming round in the car the next morning. When I got back to the house, she was furious. Whatever I said, she would not believe that I had lost my memory. She said she knew I had done a terrible thing that night, so terrible that I went into hiding, and now I was denying all knowledge of it.

'You are a liar.' Every time I protested my innocence, my ignorance, the same line came back in the same cold, measured tones.

It's strange. Until tonight, I had forgotten about my fall from the tree. I hadn't connected it with my memory of the old car in the woods. Somehow, as the years passed I'd invented a running-away-to-the-woods scene, the rebel child fleeing from home. Now I know it wasn't like that, and it worries me. If I can suddenly recall something I had lost for forty years, then who knows what else could come back. Maybe she was right. Maybe I did do something terrible.

'You are a liar,' I say it out loud to myself, and that feels better. It overrides her voice in my head. The coffee makes me feel good.

I join the audience, in the back row, and Calladine steps out on stage with Maurice behind him. They both look smart – in suits and ties – like salesmen.

'Thank you for coming.'

The murmur in the crowd dies down and everyone

looks at Calladine. I scan the rows of people on plastic chairs, wonder if they have any more idea than I do what this is all about. There are lots of loners, pensioners, two small groups of teenagers whispering, here out of curiosity like me, but two people stand out in particular – Petra Ware and a smart blonde woman in a business suit. Why would she come on a midweek night to a cold room in a Leisure Centre? Something about the poster must have got to her.

To my horror Calladine unrolls a blown-up print of my wide shot of Jake and Michelle's murder scene. People know what it is immediately, it has been in all the press. I see Petra Ware wince and look away. From the blurred quality of it, I guess he's taken it from a newspaper. He holds it up until he's sure everyone has got it, then he speaks.

'Can you explain this?' He scans the rows of chairs. 'No? Well, think. Every night, drugs change hands on our streets. Every day, families break up, kids are taken into care. This town is full of drunks and junkies. Evil begets evil. And it's just the beginning, unless . . .' He breaks off, for dramatic effect. I take a shot of him and as the flash goes off he looks furious, holding up his hand in front of his face. He stares at me, then picks up his thread.

'. . . Unless we act, now. We don't have to live in fear. Are we going to sit around while some killer plays games with letters and candles? Do you know what this painted alphabet means? Are we going to wait to find out?'

He sits down and Maurice shuffles forward nervously, clearing his throat. He opens his mouth, but before the first word can come out, the room goes black. It's windowless, so the dark seems absolute. Around me, I can hear people muttering, shifting, wondering what is going on. There is no sound from the front. Someone in the back row near me manages to stumble to the door, which they open to let in more darkness.

'Please don't leave!' There is desperation in Maurice's voice. 'We'll try to find out what the problem is.'

But the meeting was strange enough before the lights went out, and with the prospect of holding it in total darkness, I can hear chairs sliding, footsteps making for the door.

'Wait!' This time it's Calladine's voice from the front. 'There is a man here who feels responsible for the death of someone close to him. There's a woman here whose husband has left her.'

The shuffling stops.

'You know who you are. Now come to me. You can be free. You don't have to live like this.'

I can hear the sound of people sitting down again. I can just make out the shapes of others hovering near the door. A few are still leaving.

'Don't believe that this is just a blown fuse.' Calladine's voice is softer now. 'There are powers out there who don't want you to hear me, who don't want you to change your lives. Ignore them. Fight them. They mean you harm, not good. Please sit down again.'

I don't know what he's talking about, but I know I don't like it. Maurice isn't saying anything now. He is just listening like me, like everyone.

'There's a woman here with a secret.'

'Oh, come on! I can do that!' Calladine has a heckler. I recognise the voice. It is Jake's friend TJ. 'Yeah, yeah, yeah, someone sad, someone with a dead mother, someone with a secret, yeah, yeah!'

'Why did you come here?' Calladine's voice is calm, almost too quiet to hear from the back. TJ doesn't answer.

'Did you come because of Jake?'

'Don't pull your tricks on me!' TJ's voice is louder, shakier. His chair scrapes back and the door slams against the wall as he leaves.

'I'll be at the front here,' Calladine picks up as if TJ was never there.

There is murmuring, and then almost everyone starts to leave. When the lights come on again, a few people are waiting to talk to Calladine. The whole thing suddenly seems ridiculous. He is in earnest face-to-face discussion with the smart-looking woman I saw earlier. She looks haunted. His hands are on her shoulders as he speaks to her, very quietly. I wonder if she is the woman with a secret. Maurice is sitting on the edge of the stage, swinging his legs like a schoolboy. He is smiling at the punters. Two teenage boys walk up to him.

'I've got a question.' They are both smirking. 'What does the H stand for, in Jesus H. Christ?'

I take a shot of Maurice, and another of Calladine and the smart woman, then I leave.

I like losing myself in details, forgetting myself. The shape of a car on a print as I take it out of the darkroom tray – the pattern in the crushed metal that takes on a life of its own, separate from the car, the road, the crash, separate from the photograph, just a pure form, like a mood. I heard on the radio that the sun can ring like a bell. The sun, pulsing with its own energy. Why would the sun chime? No one hears it. It's the same with these details – the shape of a crashed car, a crow in the background of a shot, picking at the grass verge, the rainbow sheen of a petrol spill on a hot road. If you stand back from the human facts – the crash, the cost, the damage – then you see the beauty in the details, and it's my job to bring that out.

Somehow, now the story of the painted letters was out in the open, I didn't have to wonder what they meant. Everyone else was doing that. I could enjoy them purely for their colour, for the element of surprise in their placing. Since the D appeared on my car, I felt safer. I'd been touched by it – whatever it was – and I'd survived, so now it couldn't do me any harm. I went out looking for the F like a collector. I had to photograph them all now. My eye was sensitive to the particular scarlet of the paint, and I kept glimpsing it in shirts, discarded crisp bags, shop windows. I felt like an orchid hunter, blinded by a wealth of colours in my quest for a certain shy flower.

So when I found the G, curled around the base of a statue like a hook, I was delighted and dismayed. I photographed it, tight and wide, to show Britannia cradling a dying soldier in her arms, covering his face with her long hair. It didn't cross my mind to wonder why the G was on a war memorial, or how the town might react to that. All I felt was glad to find it, and worried that it meant I'd missed the F.

I come in late one night from a job. It's been the worst kind – an hour spent cruising up and down the motorway and no sign of a smash. What's going on? Are the police making up stories on the radio to amuse each other? I can hardly ring in and check, so I come home and make some coffee.

The more coffee I drink tonight, the more wound up I feel. I switch my radios off. If the police are telling lies I don't want to listen, even though it's my favourite voice on duty tonight.

I feel like settling scores, so I go down the hall and knock on Calladine's door. No reply. I never had my say about him using me to make posters for his meeting. I never had my say about him practically assaulting Alex in my flat, and risking my career. Since the Leisure Centre meeting, I've heard a lot of coming and going from his flat, a lot of earnest conversations. He's recruiting. Whatever he has in mind, he's recruiting for it.

With my ear pressed against the door, I can make out the pattern of his voice. I'm annoyed that he's not opening the door. Who's he talking to? I knock again. I knock and knock. Eventually the door is snatched open. He looks like he wants to kill me, but his voice says, 'Perry, come in . . .'

His flat is hot, airless. There's an open bottle of whisky and a couple of half-full glasses on the green baize table. Calladine shuts the door and walks over to the window. He stands there with his back to me. Opposite his empty seat at the card table is the smart-looking woman from the Wednesday meeting. She's in the same formal clothes, as though she's come straight from work. Her jacket is slung over the back of her chair and her face looks flushed. Some buttons of her shirt are undone.

'I'm sorry, I—'

'What d'you want?' He interrupts me, still staring out of the window. The woman says nothing. She doesn't even look up.

'I wanted a word . . .'

'It's not a good time.'

As I turn to leave, I catch sight of her eyes. They look wet and raw. My foot catches a leg of the card table and the whisky jumps in the glasses. I reach out to steady the bottle, but knock it with the ends of my fingers. The woman stands up, coughing and brushing whisky off her clothes.

'I'd better go.' She grabs her jacket, still without looking at me.

'I'm so sorry. I'm really sorry . . .' But she leaves the flat without another word. Calladine has his back to the window now, and he's staring at me. I pick up the bottle, brush the whisky from the surface of the green baize, dry my hand on my shirt.

'Get out.'

He turns back to face the window. As I shut his door behind me, I think I can hear him crying. I stand outside the door to listen, but I can't be sure.

*

That car – the car that saved me – protected me forever after that night in the woods. It became my true home. I slept and sometimes took meals at my grandmother's house, but the rest of the time that Austin Cambridge was my base and my refuge. On summer afternoons it was full of the smell of warm leather, and I couldn't stay awake in it.

The body remembers, even when the mind forgets. As I left Calladine's flat and heard him crying, I felt a presence on the back of my left hand, strong but not unpleasant, like a painless bruise. I looked at the hand and there was nothing there, but then his crying shaded into hers, and the painless bruise became the dead cold print of my grandmother's hand on mine.

She had never been to the car before. I didn't even realise she knew about it. She'd never touched me before, never hit me or kissed me or patted me on the back. Until that moment I'd assumed she wasn't quite physical. I felt that every day her age was pulling her further and further from the world. She moved around the house like a ghost. When we crossed on the stairs I felt as though I could walk right through her. At mealtimes, I was transfixed by her hands – translucent, marbled blue with blood – their skin as weak and thin as plum skin.

I don't know what shocked me most. She was in the passenger seat of my secret car, she was crying quietly, and she was reaching across into the back seat with her hand resting on mine. As I woke up I instinctively pulled my hand away, but I could still feel the chill print of hers. The car felt very small, and I was trapped. There was no way out but through her. She told me I was going back to live with my mother, and she said she was sorry. She said she would miss me. She said she knew she'd been strict with me, but she was trying to protect me.

I looked at her, but I felt as though my mouth was stitched shut. My teeth were locked together. I wanted her out of my car. I wanted her to stop talking. I turned my head away and watched her old dog half-heartedly chasing its tail among the fallen leaves.

I don't need the police radio tonight, because I'm driving past and I see it happening. He makes no attempt to keep it quiet. When I get there, he's waiting for me, waiting for me and the police.

'Go on, take me.' He poses awkwardly, with his airgun cradled in front of his chest like a great fish he's just landed. He is showing me the evidence.

'What have you done TJ?'

He is dressed in his desert war fatigues. Behind him every window on the front of Sligo's father's bungalow is shot through. I can just see Sligo's father in pyjamas, picking across the broken glass towards the window. He peers out.

'Are you all right Mr Sligo?' He is too deaf to hear me. TJ doesn't even turn around to look at him. He cocks the gun over his shoulder and fires backwards towards the voice of the old man. The shot zips off a wall and I don't think Sligo's father even hears it. He just turns around and shuffles back into the shadows.

'You could have killed him.'

'So? Take my picture.' He poses again.

'I don't want to take your picture.'

'Take it, you bastard.'

'Why?'

'I want everyone to know that I did this for Jake.'

'What? Shot an old man's windows? Is that what real soldiers do?'

TJ says nothing, just stares at me then slowly folds as if he's been hit. He sits down and lays the gun beside him. Inside the house, among the shadows of the dark living room, is the dancing glow of a TV screen.

Night work is best. Weegee taught me that, with his blinding close-up flat-pan flash. Sometimes, he couldn't see what his subjects were up to, in the shadows of an alley, or an unlit boulevard, but he'd run in to his pre-focussed ten feet, then hit the button.

His accident work taught me a big lesson – always look behind you. He's got a night shot of a New York car smash where a bread van met a car on a dimly lit street. By Weegee's standards, he's a little late, there's a bunch of people milling round, and the police are taking statements.

He takes the head-on shot first, frames it beautifully. Centre frame is a man's body, arms and legs akimbo. Two cops are standing by his head, talking and pointing. Right of frame is a van saying RYE BREAD and PUMPERNICKEL ROLLS AND CAKES. Top of frame is a bunch of voyeurs, out from the bars and clubs to see what's going on. Foot of frame is a scattering of bread – long loaves, round loaves, rolls, crackers. It's a page one shot all right, a classy piece of work.

But then – and this is the genius – he goes looking for the other car, and he finds it in the next street. There's no light here, so he takes a chance, moves into his ten-foot range and shoots. When he gets into the darkroom, what has he got? He's got a woman – white as a ghost in the dazzling flash – parked up and staring through the windscreen. She's on her way to, or from, a party by the looks of things – loose flowery dress and a big paper bloom pinned to the side of her hair. Her mouth is open, like it's full of ashes. A couple of minutes ago, she was humming the dance tunes. Now, one careless moment later, she's killed a man who was doing his job, giving New Yorkers their daily bread.

Now it's part of my routine to look behind me, to scour the place before I leave. I get the obvious shots first, but then I go hunting. In Weegee's day in a busy city how fast were these crashes – 30, 40 mph? I'm stepping into the aftermath of 80, 90 mph smash-ups, and when that happens, you have to look a little harder.

Tonight, I pick up a police call for a potential fatal near the airport link. I get there first, and get the front-end shots. There is surprisingly little blood, but an overturned lorry and an unmarked dead driver in the cab. There is still one lane open, a steady stream of rubbernecking drivers crawling past the scene. I'm about to go, but I remember my lesson – look around. Besides, it doesn't add up. There is no sign of what turned the truck.

I run back to the tunnel under the motorway. It clearly isn't blocked, because the headlights are still snaking through it. But I see a faint glow in the service tunnel next to it. This is much narrower, kept free for the maintenance teams. I follow the glow, and a hundred yards inside that tunnel is one of those souped-up hatchbacks, sideways on, with the driver on the bonnet. A team of engineers would have struggled to wedge that thing down there, but sheer speed and chance achieved it in an instant. I shoot it and make my way home through the edgelands, so pleased with myself for looking that little bit harder, and reassured that I haven't lost my stomach for the work after all.

At night, stripped of people, the edgelands is a forgotten kingdom. Now, coming home from a successful hunt, it feels like my kingdom. I slow down and open the window as I pass the buzz of the electricity sub-station, the rows of identical delivery vans asleep outside their depots.

I glimpse some movement in the huge floodlit pools of the railway yard. I stop the car, grab the camera, and make my way across the grass. I guess it's the graffiti boys. I've been waiting to catch them. I admire their work. In the last year they've turned three old restaurant carriages into one great psychedelic mural.

There's some noise, a scuffle and a shout. I fix the telephoto lens and pull focus. It's a fight. Two young graffiti artists – one still holding his spray can – are being beaten up by a pair of older teenagers. One of the lads is on the ground, and the teenagers are kicking him. An older man steps in and pulls them back, but he's not come to the rescue. He's been watching from behind. The teenagers grab one of the lads each, holding them in armlocks. As the older man shouts at them, jabbing a finger, I recognise the teenagers. They were at the Leisure Centre meeting. They were the ones who asked Maurice about the H in Jesus H. Christ.

The older man snatches the paint can from one of the lads and sprays their faces blue with a single blast each. The lads are in armlocks, so there's nothing they can do except wince, screw up their eyes and scream.

The blue-faced boys are released, staggering terrified out of the yard up towards me. I crouch down and start to run back to my car, but with my last look through the lens I see the older man – Maurice – turn to face me as he shouts after them. I don't know if he sees me.

VII

It's two nights since I broke up Calladine's soirée with that woman. He's getting to me now. I don't like him, and I don't know what he's up to. He attacks my job, tells me what pictures I can put up in my flat. Then he gets his gang to beat up a couple of graffiti artists. If that's his idea of sorting the town out, then I want nothing more to do with him.

I fix myself some food and watch the sun sink over the edgelands. All quiet on the police radios. It's my favourite voice on duty again, but she's hardly got anything to say tonight. I'm asleep in my chair when there's a knock at the door. If this is Calladine, I'm going to tell him straight. Whatever he's up to, wherever he thinks he's going, I'm not going with him. I open the door. It's not him. It's Maurice, holding two glasses and a bottle of whisky.

'Can I come in, Perry?'

'No you can't.'

'Why not?'

'Because it's late. Because I'm tired. Because you beat up young boys . . .'

'Why are you so angry, Perry?'

He puts a foot in the door, but I'm not letting him in. He tells me Calladine was upset about the other night, when he was so close to winning that woman.

'Winning her?' I'm trying not to laugh.

'We're talking about souls here, Perry.' He stares straight at me. 'Martyn's wondering whose side you're on.'

'Whose side?'

'We are God's anointed. But evil can be very persuasive.'

I slam the door in his face and hear the sound of shattering glass as the bottle hits the tiled floor outside my flat.

'Big mistake.' I hear Maurice talking to himself on the other side of the door. I spend a long time listening to the voice-beautiful on the radio. She's trying to comfort me. She doesn't think I'm evil. As the night goes on, she gives me work to encourage me – two motorway fatals in the space of an hour – but I don't go out. I don't want to leave the flat.

The only time I ever wanted to be a painter, not a photographer, was when I first saw the Unpainted Pictures. They were watercolours, the most beautiful colours I'd ever seen. At art school, I barely picked up a brush – it was always a camera for me – but when I saw the Unpainted Pictures in a book, it almost turned me around. If the real colours were anything like as bright as the pictures in the book, they must have been dazzling.

It was the story, as much as the paintings, that got to me. A German artist – I forget his name – got on the wrong side of the Nazis. Hundreds of his canvases were burnt. So he set up a secret room in a house miles from anywhere. From that room he could see all approaching roads. He thought of everything, even painting in watercolours rather than oils so the smell wouldn't give him away.

When the Gestapo came to check on him, they found an old man living quietly in the middle of nowhere, tending his vegetable garden. Forbidden to paint, he called his paintings the Unpainted Pictures. I messed about with paint for a while after that, but came back to my lenses. Ever since, I've seen my darkroom as the hidden place where work is done. Like him, most of my work is public, but I have my secret pictures too. Like his watercolours, they are things of great forbidden beauty.

I'm starting to think of my shots of Jake and Michelle as Untaken Photographs. It's time to put them with the others in a place of safety. Ever since that reporter came snooping, I've been worried about the negatives. I lock and bolt the door of the flat, then lock myself in the darkroom. I take out the envelope with the murder-scene negs and put it on the floor. The envelope stays sealed. I don't want to look at them again. With a screwdriver, I prise up a floorboard, reach down, and pull out my cashbox. As soon as it's open, I'm in a sweat. My stomach's like a fist again.

Despite all that, they are still beautiful, the old Untaken Photographs. It's the detail, the light on her skin as it breaks the surface of the water, weed across her forehead like a witch's hair, and wide shots of her body bloated with water, clothes as tight as bandages. I put them back in the box, then lay Jake and Michelle's envelope on top of them. The box is shut, floorboard nailed, and ten minutes later I'm calming down, listening to my radios again. No Gestapo, no tell-tale odours, just my Untaken Photographs. Nolde, that was it. Nolde. After the war, he repainted all his work in oils. I've never understood that.

I think of Nolde when I go out for an early morning call to the motorway. It's foggy and the radio tells me there's money to be made. As I unlock my car, I notice an envelope clamped under the windscreen wiper. I slit it open with my finger. Inside is a beautiful picture, like a watercolour, but there's no water in it. It's the Empire Pool. I recognise the ultramarine tiles, and I can just make out the silver handrail of the steps up to the diving board. The pool's been drained, and on its tiled floor is a red-painted letter F.

Several weeks, and two letters on, and I've come to no harm from the D on my car. The opposite, in fact. He – I can't quite bring myself to call him Adam today – seems to want to keep me alive. Whatever his reason for painting this alphabet, he wants it documented, and wants it publicised. If I miss a letter, he gives me a photograph of it. It helps me make a living, but it doesn't help me sleep. I worry that he's making me collaborate, that somehow I'm getting drawn in.

If I tear up his print of the F, will he give me another one? If I stop looking for the letters, will he post them through my door one by one, so I can sell them to the papers? I decide to back off. I'll keep hunting for the letters, but I won't sell my shots. If he wants publicity, he'll have to handle it himself.

*

It's an interesting test of muscle-memory. I haven't been swimming for twenty years at least. As I step through the footbath onto the poolside, I wonder if I'm going to drop like a rock. I must look uncertain, because the lifeguard has his eye on me. I recognise him – one of Jake's friends – but he doesn't know me. Once I'm in the water I feel a bit better. It's more familiar than I'd feared. I start swimming widths, and it's all coming back to me, so I try a length. It's freezing at first, then, once I'm used to it, I hold my nose and duck under. Nothing. Nothing but pure ultramarine.

In the course of half an hour, I study every blue tile on the floor of that pool, and there isn't a trace of red, never mind a letter F. I climb out and try to make conversation with the lifeguard. I ask him how often they drain the pool. I ask him if they have any problems with vandalism or graffiti. He doesn't know. He just turns up and does his lifeguard bit. I'd like to ask more, but he turns away, and he won't catch my eye.

I jump back in the pool. My mind is playing tricks on me. The touch of a hand, as a swimmer passes close, becomes her dead, trailing fingers. The man sweeping his wet hair from his face becomes her face, still and swollen, dressed with weed. I should never have looked at those pictures again. I leave quickly, before the Empire Pool becomes the pond behind her house, but it is too late. The Untaken Photographs have re-awoken something, and the only way I know to put it back to sleep is to lose myself in work, to make so many new pictures that I push hers back, drown them in a sea of strong, new images.

*

The Sligo bungalow is on my way back from the shops, so I always look. This time, after TJ's job on the windows, I'm intrigued to see how it looks in daylight. It's all been done, all boarded up. I'm glad. I was wondering if the old man would just leave it. I get out of the car and walk right around the place.

Every single window has a board instead of glass, and every single board is covered in graffiti. Some of it is the usual stuff – spray-painted signatures, initials of football teams – but some isn't the usual stuff at all. HOUSE OF BASTARDS, SCUM, SLIGO MUST DIE. You can't kill someone if you can't find them, so I guess they mean the old man. I assume he's been moved away for safety, and that's why they haven't replaced the glass. I ring the doorbell, just to make sure. I take a couple of steps back when the door opens on a security chain. The old man peers out, blinking at the daylight.

'What d'you want?'

'I . . . I've got some food if you need it.'

'There's a woman who does that.'

I hold up my bag of supplies and the door shuts. It opens again almost immediately and he lets me in. If I'd been him, I'd have left the door locked. It opens straight into the living room, in which the only light is the TV's glow. A row of sullen teenagers stares out of the screen above the catchline SHE'S CHEATING ON ME. The volume is close to deafening. A studio audience is baying and heckling. Under my feet, the carpet feels rough. I look down and realise I'm standing on shattered glass.

'Did no one clear the broken windows for you?'

He doesn't hear me. He's gone back to his armchair in front of the TV. I gesture for him to turn the volume down, but he takes no notice. I take out a packet of biscuits, open them, and put them on the arm of his chair. He doesn't look up from the TV but takes one and starts to eat.

I ask him where I'd find a broom. He doesn't reply. In the kitchen, I open a few cupboards until I find one. Then I sweep all the glass up against the wall. In another cupboard I find some thick candles. It crosses my mind to ask the old man if the candles are his or Adam's, but I know I won't get any sense out of him.

There's too much glass to pick up, but at least if it's swept aside he won't be walking on it. I do the same in the bathroom, his bedroom. Why hasn't Petra done this on any of her visits? Maybe she wants to punish him after all. I push open the last door, knowing it must be Adam's room.

The bed's unmade, as if he's just got up to get his breakfast. On the bedside table is a blister pack of tablets and a half glass of water with a surface carpeting of dust. There's a framed black and white photo of a woman, his mother I guess, holding a baby, and next to it is a beautiful framed pencil drawing of the same picture. Assuming Sligo did the drawing, he's a talented boy. There's more of his work on the walls too – strange, Gothic images of warriors and demons, with flame instead of hair, serpents' eyes and dripping fangs. Around the edge of the biggest of these pictures is a kind of runic writing, like a code or a curse. On the wall at the side of his bed is what looks like an astro-logical chart. From the ceiling, plastic model aircraft hang on cotton threads – Messerschmitt chasing Spitfire chasing Junkers – a dogfight formation pinned up years ago and left. There are piles of clothes on the floor, including a camouflage jacket and trousers under the window, covered in glass. I shake them out, and sweep the glass into a corner.

Turning round to leave the room, my heart trips as I glance at the wall above his bedhead. There, in the middle of a collage of American cars and heroes cut from magazines and adverts, is an Auburn. Not any Auburn, but an 851 ivory open-topped 1933 model, parked by a flying boat at Calshot Spit. The elegant couple with their Pekinese dogs have been scissored away to leave just the car and the plane. I feel it like a loss. My own Auburn picture can never mean the same again. I've always had a big thing for Americana. My body was born in small-town England, but my soul hails from Manhattan. Maybe Sligo is the same.

I rip his Auburn out of the collage, screw it up and throw it on the heap of broken glass. Several other cars come with it. I'm so shaken that I almost miss the montage of faces in the middle of the collage. Cheek by jowl with Marlon Brando, Elvis, Evel Knievel, is a badly taken shot of a girl. It's slightly blurred, over-exposed, but clear enough to see a girl with some trees or bushes behind her, smiling at the camera, clear enough to see that it's Michelle. I tear it off the wall and pocket it. So Sligo has some Untaken Pictures too. The door opens and his father peers into the room.

'What are you doing in here?'

'Just clearing up the glass.'

'D'you know whose room this is?'

'Adam's?'

For a moment, he looks desperate, then he turns back to the living room. On my way out, I try to show him the rest of the food, but he's not listening. The studio audience whoops as the strap-line changes to I'M SLEEPING WITH YOUR BEST FRIEND. Looking at the old man's face, I can't decide if he's totally lost in the world of TV, or totally absent from it, glazed and trapped inside his own head. I shut the front door and take my camera bag from the car. I get a good wide shot of the front of the house – boarded and graffitied – then a few close-ups round the back. The picture editors like a choice.

Night after night I'm still waking up washing my hands. I don't need to read the pop psychology in newspapers to know this isn't good. I read those columns for amusement, and to spite the ghost of my grandmother. Psychologists, priests, teachers, she was adamant that none could be trusted. All were fakes, in it for money and power. She'd have a newspaper delivered every morning, then forbid me to look at it. She didn't hide it, but left it on the kitchen table, to try to catch me out. She didn't read much of it herself, since she didn't trust journalists. But she always read the horoscopes.

Even then, I remember thinking this was odd – the queen of mistrust reading her stars every day. Once, and only once, I raised it with her. She sat me down and lectured me. Horoscopes were different. They relied on huge physical forces, not the whims and power play of men. If the tiny moon could pull the ocean tides in and out, then how much more could huge stars tug and sway our lives? It was the first time I'd heard her put her trust in anything. She was Cancer the crab. I liked that. She told me I was Pisces, but I didn't respond.

That night I was awake for hours, leaning out of my bedroom window. It was summer and the sky was clear and full. I tested what she'd told me, by looking at the brightest stars and trying to sense the pull or push of them, some kind of magnetism twisting my thoughts, forming a blueprint for the next day of my life. They were beautiful, and I saw all kinds of patterns in them, but I didn't feel a thing.

From that moment, I had mastered her. My resolve was stronger. She – who claimed she trusted no one – trusted conmen with star charts. I didn't trust astrologers, and I didn't trust her. I was the strong one. That night, the pupil overtook the teacher. My mastery of mistrust was complete.

I'm relishing the memory of that night, and the water's spilling over and over my hands. As I turn the tap off and shake the drops into the sink, I realise that I'll never wash it clean. The feeling that drives me to water night after night is the touch of her hand on mine, the only tender touch she ever gave me, an unbearable bruise that never fades, a feeling of utter revulsion.

It's afternoon. Hot and heavy. All my windows are wide open, though I'm sneezing and coughing. I don't get hay fever, until now. I can't work. I can't think straight.

The phone rings. Alex asks after my health, telling me I sound full of a cold.

'No, it's fine.'

'Have you seen an F or a G yet?'

'Not a trace.'

'You know we want to run with this.'

'I haven't seen another letter.'

The more he pesters, and the less he trusts me, the more determined I am to keep any letters to myself. I fob him off with shots of old man Sligo's boarded-up bungalow. My flat is quiet. All my radios are off. I can't bring myself to go out, so I don't want to know what I'm missing. Once or twice I hear sirens, and think of the money I could be making, but I spend the afternoon with my old treasure – a forty-year-old Swiss monorail camera.

As soon as I left college, I got caught up in photo-journalism. My old camera went into its case and stayed there. It's the opposite of everything I need for my job. It's slow, heavy, expensive to use, but it makes prints as delicate as paintings.

As a student, I made a bit of a name for myself as a still-life photographer. I spent hours gathering and arranging objects – fruit, shells, pewter, bone – and getting the light just right, before I even thought of setting up the camera. Now I haven't got the patience for that. I take the camera out of its wooden case and find – to my delight – one sheet of virgin film left loaded in the dark slide.

I set up the camera on its tripod by the window where the light is good. I search the kitchen. No apples, no onions, nothing natural to work with. In the cupboard there's a tin of sardines. I rinse off the red sauce and arrange them – four headless silver fish – on a white plate. I put them on the table under the window and frame up.

It takes a long time, turning the plate, nudging it in and out of the sunlight, shadow, half-shadow, full sun, framing really close and detailed until the patina of the scales is perfect, sharper than reality. When I'm finally settled on the light, the arrangement of the fish, the framing of my one shot, I trip the shutter, and the exposure is made.

I take it straight into the darkroom, and conjure four fish from a single sheet of paper. When it's all done, I take it out – still drying – into the living room, and place it on the table next to the plate of sardines. There's no doubt in my mind that the photograph is stronger – more accurate, more real. I examine every detail, and I notice textures on my monochrome fish that simply weren't visible on the originals. They are more beautiful.

I sit in the armchair facing the open window, letting the noise outside float me into sleep. I dream of swimming in the Empire Pool, but every time I ground my feet they land on something jagged, sharp, like broken pots or shells. Finally, I take a breath and duck under the surface. To my horror, the ultramarine tiles are crawling with huge crabs – terracotta coloured – snapping and scuttling. The only way to keep my feet away is to swim, but the pool is edgeless – no bars, no steps – just an endless rippling surface, catching the light on every wave-tip.

VIII

It was the smoke that woke me up. I always slept with my window open, so when the smell of burning cut into my sleep, I got out of bed and looked out. I remember – even at that most shocking moment – I remember thinking '*this was always going to happen*'.

I didn't rush to the door, or scramble for my clothes. I just watched a grey tail of smoke fanning out above the woods, and I knew the car was lost. In my memory now I can sift the elements of the smoke – the stench of burning rubber from the tyres, the leather of the seats, the dried-up residues of oil from the rusted engine. But I think that's a trick of the memory.

On the night itself, I think smoke was all I could smell, smoke that stayed in my head for days – every time I breathed in – to remind me of what I'd lost. The worst thing, though I didn't have to see it to know it, was that fleeting glimpse of my grandmother hurrying back across the garden, as if she was escaping the first drops of a rainstorm. As she reached the back door, I recall – though this could be memory's tricks again – I recall her eyes flicking up to meet mine.

I steer well clear of Calladine now. He'll go through phases when he's out of the flat all day, and Paddy barks and barks. Then he'll have days like this, when there's a steady stream of visitors up the stairs. I'm making an effort to get back to work. I've got the radios on and I'm waiting for a job that's worth the trip. I make coffee in the most complicated way I can – beans, grinder, filters, the lot – because I like the ritual. Halfway through the process, the doorbell rings. I've been expecting a visit from God's Anointed for days. I know they won't leave me alone. I just hope they don't bring spray cans or baseball bats. But it's not them at the door, it's TJ.

'I just wanted to thank you.'

'For what?'

'You know.'

I don't. He's still very intense. I don't like being too close to him. I can't understand how he's here, shaking my hand, why he isn't in custody for trying to shoot the old man. That night at Sligo's house I decided not to take him at face value. When I asked him if shooting old men was what real soldiers do, he looked at me as if he'd been rumbled. Now he looks like he's got his confidence back.

'If you'd taken that photo when I asked you, I'd have been in big trouble.' Now he's making me feel uneasy. I stand in the doorway so he doesn't think he's invited in.

'I was spared, you know, spared to work for right-eousness. God told the old man to say nothing, to forgive me.'

'Where did you learn to talk like that?' I know, of course. My heart sinks as I hear it.

'I told Martyn when I joined that I'd stop wearing

this gear.' He holds open his combat jacket, looking down at his camouflage trousers and mirror-polished boots. 'But Martyn says I'm still a soldier. All I've done is switch sides. I'm a soldier of righteousness now.'

I take a step back and push the door half closed, hoping he'll take the hint. Behind his voice I'm picking up an RTA on the police radio. Not just RTA, but MULTIPLE RTA. It's too good to miss, and it's close, the closest junction to my flat. Ten minutes, out through the edgelands, up a farm track, scale the grass verge and I'm there. I'm trying to close the door, reaching for my camera bag, and he's telling me he's a soldier of righteousness.

'Martyn's told me things about myself, really important things.'

'I've got to go now, TJ.'

He's costing me minutes here. I open the door, barge past him and down the corridor. Would Weegee have stayed to talk? I'm a photographer. When the picture's there, I've got to take it.

Later that night, the rain came down, a storm. I spent hours by the window, watching the smoke tail die back, the glow of the flames fade. In the morning, my grandmother said nothing about it – the usual silent breakfast. I knew she had done it to hurt me, but I didn't want to let her know how much. I had one more week before going home to my mother, one more week of this battle of wills.

That morning the car was too hot to touch, still

steaming. I'd seen a calf born on TV, and it made me think of that, all black and steaming in its hollow of leaves and bushes. Its blue-green flaking surfaces were powdery black, the leather of the seats had split and curled and hardened. I knew why she'd put a match to it. She was destroying the evidence. That car – my car – was the place where she had cracked. She'd touched my hand. I'd seen her cry. She had to do something about it, to get her balance back. I understood all that on her terms, and I hated her even more for it.

By the next afternoon, it had cooled off enough to touch, and that evening I could get back inside. I climbed through the window and into the back seat. It was hard, even sharp in places. The stink of fire was powerful, but I lay down on the back seat as I used to, and closed my eyes. She was livid of course, but she said nothing. I walked in and across the kitchen on my way up to bed. I didn't look at her, but I could feel her stare on the back of my head. My clothes, my hair, even my face was blackened by the burnt leather. I'd rolled and rolled on the back seat to make sure of it.

There's no denying that it hit me hard. Weegee had a rare nose for a story, but he also had exceptional eyes. Unless you can see the details others miss, you might as well leave the lens cap on. So when I picked up the paper to find out if Alex had used my shots of Sligo's house, I almost gave up there and then. The story of old man Sligo imprisoned by fear in his windowless house was a mere sideshow to the revelation that the alphabet writer had struck again.

In a blown-up detail from one of my pictures – just below the word BASTARDS on a boarded-up window – was the letter H. It was obvious, bright red and painted by hand. All the other graffiti were done with spray cans. If I'd noticed the H, I'd have charged him double for the shots. But I didn't. I'd printed them up myself, and I never saw it. The paper put out a plea for readers to help find the missing F. It concluded that Jake and Michelle's killer was still in town, still playing games with the police, daubing his own home to taunt them, to show them how close he still was.

What scared me more than the alphabet was missing a crucial detail in my own pictures. I was losing my touch. Too much digging up the past. Too much interference. Too many conversations. Not enough hard solo work, alone with a camera. It was time to get back to the fundamentals.

The sun is very low, cutting through the windscreen as it was on the evening of the murders. I take the same route as I took that night, but I take it more slowly. There has been rain, for the first time in a week, and it has put a shine on all the surfaces. There is still a very fine drizzle, like mist in the air. I drive past Mister Motor's yard as he is locking the gates. He sees me and waves furiously, trying to flag me down. I shake my head and point forward at the glistening road as I pass him. The radio is on and they are still calling patrol cars up to the motorway. This must be big. I leave the car in the far corner of the Bluebird Centre's massive car park, and run down the farm track that leads off it. Just before the farmhouse, I clamber up the grass bank that leads to the motorway.

So quick, I know I'll be first on the scene. No time to waste, but I freeze at the top of the bank for what feels like minutes. The low, hard sun is perfect. I couldn't have placed it better myself. And the pictures, well, I could sell them now before I've even taken them. In front of me is a scene as intricate as a still life.

Cars are tangled in each others' wreckage, victims are bowing over steering wheels or slumped in their seats. In the front cars – the most remarkable sight – Canada geese have smashed through windscreens, lying in the laps of dead passengers like pets, or splayed on the bonnets of wrecked cars. Some survivors from the cars further back are sitting on the road, dazed, or trying to climb back in through broken windows, desperate for signs of life. Behind them, backed up as far as the eye could see, are rows of lights.

I run down the bank on to the motorway and start shooting. These are astonishing pictures. I've been working for maybe two minutes when I hear the sirens coming in the distance. Then I see the open-topped Mercedes. In the driving seat, a woman with long red hair is moaning, with her head on the steering wheel. The man next to her, a blond man in a bloodstained cream suit, has collapsed across her lap. On the bonnet of the car is a goose, almost central, with its neck and head tucked beneath its heavy brown body. I know what to do. It is pure instinct. The sirens are getting louder, so I shift the bird to the centre of the bonnet, free its neck, and arrange it across the white car. Then I reach in, pull the dead man up by his arm, and lean him back in his seat. I push the lady back into her seat, with her head settled against the side window. She's stopped moaning by now. I take my shots and leave as the police arrive.

All the way home I'm singing. I'm singing to my camera on the passenger seat, I'm singing to the film inside the camera, praising its beauty. Mister Motor has gone home, but as I pass his locked gates topped with razor wire, I congratulate myself on keeping my head down, on not pulling over to talk to him. If I'd wasted five minutes catching up with Mister M, my camera would be empty now.

By the time I get home I'm sweating rather than singing. My palms are slipping on the steering wheel and I can feel the thump of the pulse in my neck. As I get into the darkroom, my stomach clenches again. It feels like I've swallowed a rock. I prepare the trays, the chemicals, and take the film out of the camera. I'm not giving in to this feeling. Did Weegee feel sick when he printed his work? If so, we'd never have heard of him. He'd have been a taxi driver, shoe-shine, a rabbi like his dad. No, an ambulance-chaser needs a good nose, good eyes, and a cast-iron stomach. I steady myself and begin the ritual.

I stop for a moment – and this is my mistake – to switch the darkroom radio from police band to news channel. FIFTEEN CONFIRMED DEAD, AND MANY SERIOUSLY INJURED IN MOTORWAY PILE-UP. I switch it off and make myself focus on the trays, the negatives, on my work. I keep thinking about that arrow of geese aimed at the wet motorway – perhaps mistaking it for a river – and below, a smart couple in a soft-top Mercedes, listening to jazz as they discuss the night ahead. I imagine his smashed-up face made whole again, his tongue clicking to the beat of the music. Then there he is in the tray in front of me, his disfigured face seen through a windscreen with a broken-necked goose in the foreground.

I did set it up to perfection. It looks like the paintings we studied at college – it has weight, perspective, the lot. Even the way I propped his arm on the back of her seat echoes the shape and arch of the bird's neck curled like a black snake on the white of the car. I watch my hands take the print out of its bath and tear it in half, then tear it again and again, until the pieces are too small to rip. Then they take some scissors, and shred the negatives. Then they tip the trays down the sink. Then they open the darkroom door, lead me out, and shut it behind me. Only then do they stop shaking. I go to the bathroom and throw up.

That night I was on the riverboat again, arriving at the same Ashanti village. We were all dressed in white suits and dresses as before, but as we drew up at the riverside the mood was different, unsettled, even threatening. I couldn't work out why. Perhaps it was because I knew about the baby this time, knew exactly what the villagers were passing down the ceremonial line. I joined that line as I had done before, and as before the only available space was right by the water. Again,

I looked down at my shoes – those chestnut brogues – with the river lapping over them. As I looked, the water became streaked with green algae and long sinews of weed, which wrapped and twisted round my ankles, until I could no longer see the punched brown leather of the shoes.

Suddenly aware of a noise, I looked up to see the trees above fill with huge white storks, clacking their beaks as they nudged for space on the branches. They were all staring at us. When I looked down, I saw the bundle again, across my open arms. The baby had reached me, tightly bound in leaves held together this time by shoelaces the colour of my brogues. I glanced down the line, and all the faces were imploring me to kiss the child, to kiss her goodbye before giving her up to the river. I bowed my head, but as my lips hovered above her cheek, I noticed that the face was split, pursed, dried like old fruit. The villagers kept staring – I could feel them – but I couldn't kiss her. There was no way I could kiss her.

Next morning I wrote the dream down, then I paced around the flat for an hour or so. I didn't switch any of the radios on. There was no point in listening to the police broadcasts if I knew I wasn't going to act on anything they said. I sat down and studied the plate of sardines still left out on my dining table. Now they were melting into each other – shrivelling and drying – filling the flat with their sharp scent. I took a knife and scraped the fish muck into the bin, then I threw the plate in after it and heard it smash.

*

The Distortion Series. Why did he do it? I've weighed that one up. He builds a career from a camera set at F16 with a focal distance of ten feet. Every shot he takes is framed up ten feet out with a flash. Then he hits Tinseltown and starts messing about with lenses. He does portraits – Marilyn Monroe, Jerry Lewis – but he distorts the faces, disfigures them.

Was it a yearning to experiment, to challenge our perception of glamour and beauty? Or was it much more basic than that? I think so. He was fat and famous, but he missed the streets. He missed the night shift, the blood, the slit throats. He missed the faces of his subjects, the lost, the unlucky, the punished. He missed being Weegee.

I don't have to leave town to make my Distortion Series. I don't need special lenses either. This place is getting more warped by the day, or more precisely, by the letter. There was always a fair bit of small-town paranoia, but the presence of a ritual killer daubing some black-magic spell across the place has given everyone a fever. The whole town is edgelands now.

IX

Mister Motor left a message on my voicemail.

'I think I've found an eye.'

I play it again, about five times. It doesn't make sense, but my machine is old and it mangles the voices it records. I drive down and park in the bays reserved for customers. Next to me, a Jaguar pulls in, a man in a suit gets out. He looks like a bank manager. He tells his wife to stay in the car. His face is flushed and he's muttering to himself. I follow him into Mister M's reception and he kicks off, shouting about his wife leaving her car for a couple of minutes, only to find it gone when she got back. Mister M barely looks up from the sports page, reminds the man that his wife had parked on a double yellow line.

I get a coffee from the machine in the corner. The bank manager starts gripping and shaking the bars between him and Mister M. He's shouting about a doctor's appointment, how his wife can't walk far so she had to park outside, how she only took a few minutes. Above him across the bars is a sign saying £50 RELEASE FEE ALL CARS.

I'm sipping at my burning black coffee. Mister M is flicking the pages of his newspaper. The bank manager is using words he doesn't use in front of his clients. Mister M lets him rant until the storm has blown itself out, then speaks.

'That's fifty quid please, sir.'

Quietly, the bank manager gets out his cheque-book and asks to borrow a pen. He's still muttering under his breath. Mister M calls his son from the back room, to take the bank manager to his wife's car. He notices me and nods. The cheque is handed over, and the bank manager leaves. I tell Mister M he deserves a round of applause. He smiles. I say my machine was playing up, so I didn't get the meaning of his message. He tells me he's found an eye, and says he'll show me.

I follow him out to the stacked wrecks at the back where he'd met Sligo. On the way, the man in the Jag nearly cuts us down. His wife, in a little red soft-top, glides past looking sheepish.

'There. What d'you think?'

'Sorry?'

'There, on the side of that blue van.'

He asks me if I've brought my camera. He thinks there's money in this.

'It's bright, not true scarlet, and it's spray painted.'

'So?'

'That's not what they're like.' I tell him I'm certain it isn't the I. Since the H – my shot of the H on Sligo's father's house – everyone has been looking for the I. Clearly, someone thought they'd have a go at making it. It even crossed my mind that Mister M himself had got the spray can out, but I don't think he would stoop to that. His son is standing by the office looking over at us.

'Look, I'm really sorry, but I've seen all the letters.'

I can see he is crestfallen. He shrugs, and we turn

away from the fake I, heading back to the office. As we walk in, Mister M's son raises an eyebrow.

'Well?'

White is not a big colour in my wardrobe at the best of times. This summer I'm rooting in the wardrobe and drawers for the darkest clothes I can find. If I can look like an undertaker, so much the better. Anything that puts a bit of distance between me and the cult across the corridor.

At first, I noticed Calladine and Maurice wearing white suits. A little old-fashioned, perhaps, but hey, it's summer. Now I see nothing but white coats, white dresses, white overalls coming up and down the stairs. I met TJ in the hallway one morning, and made the mistake of asking him why.

'We dress in white to show that we're on the side of light, against darkness. A darkness has fallen on this town, and we have to break it.'

It didn't even sound like TJ. It sounded like a man rehearsing a line he didn't fully understand.

'What the fuck?' I didn't know what else to say.

Mister Motor shoos his son out of the office. He looks anxious. There is someone banging on the counter outside, rattling the bars – another angry driver. He sends his son to deal with it, and shuts the door. I feel bad. That phoney letter I must have meant a lot to him. Perhaps he was building up his hopes of a news-paper coup, but I couldn't lie. Whoever is painting the letters, they are doing it with a brush and scarlet paint, not with a spray can.

'Look, about that letter, I'm sorry, but—' He stops me in my tracks, brushing it aside.

'Forget it. Look there's something else.'

So he goes back to talking about Adam Sligo. It's quite a coincidence. I've been wanting to talk about him too. Apart from Jake and Michelle, Mister M's the only one who's seen Sligo since he left home weeks ago, and Jake and Michelle aren't saying anything. I interrupt him.

'These letters. Why d'you reckon Sligo's doing them?'

'Playing scrabble with the police?' He shrugs.

Outside the door, his son is shouting at the angry customer. It's hard to concentrate, with the level of abuse rising next door. He hasn't mastered his father's stonewall technique.

We can barely hear ourselves think. Mister M can't take it any longer. He throws the door open and the shouting dies down. He spells out – very quietly – that they don't have to put up with such abuse, and if the customer doesn't write a cheque in the next two minutes, he'll be writing a cheque tomorrow for a new car. The clamping and the crushing are not separate businesses, he says, they go well together. The customer – another red-faced man in a suit – mutters a few last insults to salvage his pride, then reaches for his chequebook.

'Anthony,' says Mister M to his son, 'when you've finished with this gentleman, I'd like a word.' His son nods, looking rattled. Mister M sits down again, apologises, shakes his head.

'Tony's fault. He didn't control it.'

We start talking about Sligo again, but it's hard to pick up the thread. Mister M's rambling a bit, telling me how sad Sligo looked when he found him in the driver's seat of that wrecked car, how he had talked about his mother, about Mum, Mum, Mum . . .

'You said there was something else you haven't told me before?'

'Yes, yeah . . .'

Anthony is with us now, standing looking anxious with his back against the closed door.

'Look,' says Mister M, 'I've got to go, but it's just . . . he kept talking about Michelle too. Not just his mum but Michelle, saying her name and asking if she was okay.'

'He kept saying Michelle?'

'Michelle and Mum. It was weird.'

Anthony butts in.

'Michelle wouldn't have anything to do with him! None of the girls would go near him!'

Mister M looks as if he's going to hit Anthony. I tell him I have to go. Mister M walks me out of his yard. I'm thinking of Michelle's photo on Sligo's wall, but I'm not telling him. He leaves me at the gate, to go and deal with his son. I turn to watch him walk away – tall, thin, always in oily dark blue overalls. I glance up, my eye taken by something bright. Then I burst out laughing. Mister M hears me, and looks round. I point to the arched iron sign above his gates. The I of MISTER MOTOR has been overwritten in scarlet paint. The colour is right, the brushwork. It's as clear as a signature.

*

Distortion Series – Image One: Nirvana nightclub. Early hours of Saturday morning. Three lads lying beaten in an alley by the side of the club. Two hospitalised, one treated at the scene. Rumour is, they were pushing pills on the dance floor. Police take statements, but don't seem too interested. Dealers decline to press charges. Eyewitnesses talk about three men with baseball bats, all in identical white tracksuits.

I circle the big interchange roundabout on the outer fringe of the edgelands. This used to be my office, my bank, my gateway, my vocation. I was the king of the motorways.

Now I loop the huge roundabout six or seven times, stopping at various sets of lights. The lights have posters stuck to their bases, mocking me. EARN £100 A DAY WITHOUT LEAVING HOME. LOSE WEIGHT NOW, ASK ME HOW, RING 078 . . . I don't catch the rest.

I go home, park the car outside the flats and tap the rabbit's foot and horse chestnut that hang from my rear-view mirror. They swing on their strings and rap against the windscreen. They're my personal voodoo, to keep me safe, to keep my luck strong on the motorways.

I rip them from their strings and throw them in the gutter as I leave my car. How have I let it come to this?

X

I find myself thinking a lot about Paddy, the wild dog adopted by my neighbour. I like the dog, and I think he'd be better off with me, out of the way of all that white-clad madness. I want to take Paddy to the park, give him a run around, but he won't let me near him. He doesn't trust a soul except Calladine, but I'm working on it. I can win converts too.

I went back into my darkroom for the first time in weeks and conjured some shots of the I from my chemicals. Close, wide, black and white. I'd even shot a colour film. I called Alex and fixed a fee. I needed the money. He said he'd run it in colour on the front page, so everyone could see the blood-red paint. He liked that colour.

Sure enough, they ran it big. Mister Motor must have got a cheque too, since he talked about why he was 'targeted'. He told them he'd been chosen because his yard was where Sligo was last seen. He said it was Sligo's way of letting us know he was still in control. They asked Mister M if he had any clue where Sligo was. Had he dropped any hints before he left Mister M's yard? Mister M said he hadn't a clue, he thought Sligo was too clever to be caught.

Of course, that wasn't enough for the paper. They ran an editorial demanding that the hunt be stepped up and the letters stopped 'before the killer strikes again'. I tore it out and filed it with the cuttings. I got my town map out and marked the letters A to I, where I'd found them. There was no pattern, no shape, except perhaps a vague drift from east to west. I wasn't going to the motorway any more, but I was documenting the letters. I told Alex on the phone that he could rely on me. I'd missed the F, and got the H without knowing it, but from here on it was my job, and I wasn't going to miss another letter.

I was determined to keep visiting my Austin Cambridge, even after the fire. I spent whole afternoons in it, just as I had before. I hated these mind games, but she had started it, and the crucial thing was not to lose. I couldn't quite believe that she could keep up her silence about burning the car, as I walked right past her most afternoons, blackened by it. For her, it was an unspoken battle, so I played it that way. Her jaw was set, her teeth clenched. I could see that having shown some affection, some weakness towards me in the car, she would bury any tenderness so deep that it would never surface again.

My games in the car changed then. Up until the fire, it had always been a refuge. The back seat was my place, a place to lie down and let the leaves above be the sound of the road. Smooth tyres on a wet strip. I was a movie star, asleep on the back seat of my Auburn 851, being chauffeur-driven to my retreat in Calshot Spit after a hard day's filming.

Since the fire, all that had changed. The smell of leather upholstery had sharpened to a charred stench. I couldn't sleep in the back, so I became the driver. I moved to the front and took the wheel. The steering column had rusted away, so the wheel could spin in my hands. The gear lever was locked solid, but the pedals worked fine – I still went through the motions of first, second, third. I was Ab Jenkins, record-breaking racing driver. I was hired by the Auburn Automobile Company to test every new 851 to a hundred miles per hour.

In my last week there I spent all day in the car. Partly I was making a point, but partly I was getting scared of her. If love can reach beyond itself, then so can hatred. Our meals together were agony. She didn't say a word. I started to skip lunch, then dinner. She said nothing, but later I'd find the food I'd missed congealed, stuck to plates on my bedroom floor. On principle, I didn't touch them, so I lived on breakfast. I counted down the days and knew I could last the week. Hungry or not, I would not weaken.

By the end of the week I was driving for hours in the burnt-out car, across the States, New York to Los Angeles at full tilt. Ab Jenkins at the wheel on a desert road, dodging roadrunners, coyotes. When I heard the dog, it was a shock at first. Her dog was usually as silent as she was. It showed me no affection, but I didn't dislike it. It was old and tired, and slept all day. Now it was howling and yapping. The sound was coming from the side of the house, the walled garden. The dog's cries were strange, but not as strange as the next thing I heard, which made me take my foot off the gas, my hands off the steering-wheel. I remember feeling frozen, straining to hear it, but hoping it would stop. She was calling me. The woman who burnt my car, who never said a word to me, was calling me by name – shrill, getting stronger. I didn't move a muscle. She called again, five or six times. There was a note of desperation in her voice. The dog was quiet now, and she was howling, even saying 'please' after my name, begging me to come, to help her.

I restarted the engine of my Auburn 851, slipped it into first, and set off. The windows were down. It was hot in the desert. Yes, the Arizona Desert. People can die out here in the sheer blinding heat, so you have to be careful. You can't afford to stop for anyone, for anything. Keep driving.

Distortion Series – Image Two: It was done, it seems, in broad daylight. Sunday afternoon, the industrial estate is empty. The only people coming and going are visitors to the murder scene, coming with their curiosity, their hopes and fears, their soft toys and flowers.

Anyhow, between visits, sometime after lunch, the guy ropes to the awning were cut, the flowers shredded and the messages torn up.

That makes it sound more measured than it looked. It looked frenzied, with the canvas slashed to ribbons. Whoever did it was in a hurry, or a rage, or both. They tried to set light to the awning before they left, but it didn't catch. One corner of the fabric was burnt away, as if someone had taken a bite out of it.

*

I've been working on Paddy for weeks, trying to win his trust, and he's warming to me. I used to think he was going to attack me every time I went near him. He was so hostile for so long, I wondered if he knew I was the man who nearly ran him over. Now he comes up and rests his head against my leg whenever I see him in the corridor – he spends a lot of time in the corridor these days. I wake up one morning to the sound of a hammer and chisel, and find Calladine taking the lock off his front door. I guess he wants his followers to come and go as they please. Besides, with a big wild dog on guard, I guess he has no need of locks.

'Can I take him out?' I'm not sure I should ask, but his door is ajar as ever, and he can see me patting the dog.

'If he wants to.'

'Where's his lead?' Of course, there is no lead. 'D'you have a rope?'

'You won't need one. He'll walk with you.'

So he does. I call him to heel and he follows me out of the flat. Calladine runs after me and hands me two twenty pound notes.

'Pick up a couple of bottles of whisky, would you?'

It's a lot of cash for whisky.

'Decent stuff, you know.'

I feel embarrassed in the mini-mart, buying two bottles of malt in the middle of the morning. Embarrassed, and resentful of him for getting me to run his errands. I wish I'd said no, but then again, I like his dog.

I go back via the park, to give the dog a runaround,

but he doesn't want to run. We walk by the four cages that pass for a mini-zoo. The pheasants are out at the front of theirs, pecking at nothing. The rabbits are asleep, and the peacocks are weighed down by their own faded beauty. Paddy stops at the last cage, as I always do. After many visits, I've decided it's a joke. I have never had so much as a glimpse of 'The Maned Wolf', just tall grass, a few bare branches, and a ramshackle shelter at the back. At the front of the cage are a few scraggy bones.

Paddy lies flat out in the sunshine, so I sit down by him, and take a swig of the whisky. I'm as warm inside as out. I could stay there and drink myself to sleep, but Paddy nudges me, so we go.

On the way home, I see a small crowd outside All Saints Church. At first it looks like a wedding or a funeral, but no one is wearing a suit. As I get closer, I can hear hushed, earnest talk. On the oak church door is a red, painted letter J. This seems like a step up in menace. It's the biggest letter yet, stretching the full height of the door. The vicar is outside, comforting his parishioners. But he doesn't look calm himself. He touches the J, and his finger comes up with a trace of scarlet. Some of the neighbours have fetched cameras, and are snapping it. That's my job. I run back to the flat to fetch my kit, and Paddy leads the way.

XI

These days, when I see someone in white clothes, I don't think they're going to a wedding. One of my other neighbours, a fat man from the end of the landing, has taken to wearing white overalls. At first, I thought it might be a new job. In the past I've seen him in the dark blue uniform of a Bluebird Centre security guard, complete with an embroidered bird on the top of each sleeve. Then I started to see him coming and going from the flat-with-no-lock.

Trouble is, when they start wearing white, they want to talk to you. I've never had more than a nod from him before, but this morning he stops on the landing and offers me a handshake. He says his name is Che. I say I've seen him on the stairs in a uniform. He just nods, doesn't say anything about his job, but it doesn't stop him asking what I do.

'I used to be a photographer.'

'And now?'

'Not sure.'

Che tells me how Martyn's helping him, how Martyn's given him the courage to socialise for the first time in a year, how Martyn's working to transform him, but it's tough, deep-seated. I'm sick of hearing the name Martyn, so I talk about Che's name instead.

'Unusual name, yours,' I say.

'Parents were hip. I was a red baby.'

'Did you ever see that photo of your namesake?'

'I've got it on a T-shirt.' He sounds flat, reluctant.

'No, not that one. I mean the death shot – *The Death of Che Guevara.*'

'No.'

'They laid him on a cattle trough after they'd shot him. Then they sent the picture round the world to prove that he was dead.'

I leave a pause for a response, but there isn't one.

'Weird thing is his eyes. He doesn't look dead at all.'

Distortion Series – Image Three: Adam Sligo's name seems to be on everyone's lips. The longer he's mocking the town with his painted letters, mapping out his next attack – the more he is feared and admired in equal measure.

My picture is perfect, I have to say. I framed up low, crouching, so the huge armadillo shape of the Soccerdome was looming behind them. There, not quite in the foreground, were two young lads in England football shirts. They put them on as soon as they had bought them, then they set off proudly walking through the edgelands.

Although they didn't see me take a shot of them, I managed to get close enough to read the names printed on the back of their shirts. It crossed my mind for a moment that it might be their name, but what are the chances of two friends called Adam buying new shirts on the same day? Slim, I'd say.

*

It's the night after he introduced himself to me in the corridor. Che is clearly drunk, swaying at my door as if caught in a breeze. From the sounds of things in the flat across the landing, there is some kind of party going on.

'I've got something to show you.' He beckons me to follow him. I shake my head. There is no way I'm going into that party. He picks up my fears.

'It's not that. It's nothing to do with them.'

I'm still not moving.

'It's something you'll appreciate, as a photographer.'

I follow Che down the corridor towards his flat. He doesn't need a key, since the lock on his front door is chiselled away, like the lock on his master's door. If this is a cult, it must be the sort of cult where everyone shares everything. Despite the lack of security, he still has to put a shoulder to the door, then tells me to watch my feet. I step across a pile of free newspapers and advertising leaflets. I ask if he's been away, but he says he hasn't.

'D'you like my tree?'

I just laugh. In the corner of his living room is a floor-to-ceiling plastic palm tree, complete with coconuts.

'Picked it up from work when they were doing the jungle zone.'

I ask him how he got it home, but he's gone off into a bedroom and doesn't hear me. Apart from the tree, the flat seems to have no character – no pictures or books, just a sofa, TV, empty cans and pizza boxes. He comes back in brandishing a video tape.

'Sit down. Just shift that stuff onto the floor.'

'What's the tape?'

'It's a surprise.'

He feeds it into the machine, picks up the remote, and hits rewind. He takes a can of beer out of the fridge and sits down beside me on the sofa. As an afterthought, he offers me a beer, but I say no. We sit watching the blank screen, listening to the slow grind of the rewind.

'What is this, Che?'

'Patience, patience. Trust me. It's good.'

I make an excuse about feeling sick – too much food and drink – and get up to go. As I reach the door, the video clicks and settles. Che presses the remote and the tape is on.

'Come back! Come back! Just for a minute.'

The more I tried to concentrate on driving, the louder her screams seemed to get. I didn't try to imagine what was making her scream. I gripped the steering-wheel with a stranglehold, and leaned into the gear stick to try to dislodge it. I'd only heard her use my name a handful of times, each time treated like a slip of the tongue. Now I could hear her repeating it over and over. I shut my eyes and pictured the detail of the desert road. Ab Jenkins was getting hot. The sun was baking him through the wind-screen. Tumbleweed, yes, tumbleweed was rolling down the road, and the road was running out, narrowing to a track. There was a heat haze, shimmering in the distance and out of it loomed cacti the size of trees.

Leaves from the real copse dropped onto the bonnet of the burnt-out Austin Cambridge, then turned into lizards on the bonnet of the Auburn 851, great lizards flicking tails and basking. Then the coyotes appeared, running along beside the car, ducking in front of it, making me swerve, trying to make me crash. More and more of them came out of the desert to confront me. Every time I dodged one, I came face to face with another, and they were yelping, howling, calling 'Perry! Help me!' in my grandmother's voice, and it was all I could do to keep control of the car. Then suddenly the coyotes stopped howling, their chins went down, and they sloped off the road, foraging. The road was opening up again, the cacti receding to mere dots on the horizon. The heat haze was steadying, cooling and becoming clear.

I stopped the car, pulled the handbrake on, and listened. I guess I must have listened for a long time, because I started getting cold. I waited until I was shivering and needed to get indoors. I hoped the dog was okay. I don't recall the walk back from the woods to the house. I've got certain details, like snapshots – the back door standing open, the kitchen chair on its back, the magazine open at an article called TEN SYMPTOMS YOU MUSTN'T IGNORE.

I remember going upstairs, looking out of the window and seeing the dog. I didn't see her then. I got my camera for the dog. My brand new camera. Birthday present, guilt present from my mother. I'd taken two or three shots from my room, then lost interest. But this was interesting. This was a real subject. I took it out into the garden, and rattled off ten or so. I finished off the film on my old Auburn in the copse, just so I'd remember it.

I hear the video click, and I can't resist coming back to see what it is. I decide to watch the beginning, then to leave him to it, whatever it is. I walk back to the sofa and stand in front of it.

'Sit yourself down.'

Che pats the seat next to him. I shake my head without looking at him. I just keep staring at the screen. It is black and white footage of a shop – a clothes shop – with people milling around, taking outfits off rails, disappearing into changing rooms and coming out again. I'm baffled. Che looks at me and points to the screen. He is gazing at it, fascinated. I keep watching, waiting for it to make sense. After a couple of minutes, it cuts to another shop, a music shop this time, with people rifling through racks of CDs. In the foreground, there are customers with headphones on, clustered around a listening console, trying out CDs.

'Blows your mind, doesn't it?'

Che turns to me. I shrug. He carries on.

'Does that look like a man who's just murdered two people?'

'Where?'

'In the front there, with headphones on.' He gets up and taps the screen, but at that moment the footage shifts to a café with tables set out as if in some Mediterranean town square. But instead of the Mediterranean, the tables look out across a fake jungle full of plastic trees like the one in the corner. It's the Bluebird Centre. After the murders, Che had to scan all the security tapes, to see if he could trace Adam Sligo.

'There was loads of it. But hard to track. He kept stealing clothes and changing them, made a den for himself in the temple in the middle of the jungle.' He taps the screen again. 'Look, this is the next morning. He's in the Burger Bar having his breakfast now.' Che laughs. I don't look at him, I'm watching Adam Sligo, getting drawn in. Che is right. It is special. There is something about the innocence of the hidden camera, the sheer calm of the killer, his relaxed meandering from shop to shop. It's mesmerising. It makes you think. It makes you wonder if he really is the killer. There is nothing about him, no sense of panic, no quick movements, no glances side-to-side to see if he is being followed. He is a man at peace with himself.

'But he only paid with cash.' Che knocks his fore-head with his finger. 'There's thinking. Didn't want his cards traced, did he?'

'How much is there?'

I sit down. I could watch for hours. Che says there is half an hour or so – short clips from different shops. He says that when he made the compilation for the police, he ran off a copy for himself. He says he watches it a lot.

'Where did Sligo sleep?'

'Watch . . .'

Che grins and presses fast-forward on the remote control. The shoppers swarm into shops like an infest-ation. He stops it on a wide-shot of the central atrium.

Escalators slide up and down at the edge of the phoney jungle. The camera must be high up on the roof, because it's hard to see any of the faces. He freezes the frame, and points to a tiny figure looking around, then climbing over the low wall into the jungle. You can just make him out, through the foliage, entering the plastic Aztec temple in the middle. I ask him to show me again, so he rewinds, and we watch Adam Sligo disappearing into the temple, then reversing out of it, then being swallowed again.

I have to say that the J is my favourite letter so far. It was such an ideal setting, on the dark wood door of the church. The scarlet looked as shocking and dramatic as a wound. Adam Sligo has a good eye. When the papers ran my picture of the J, they launched a campaign on behalf of their readers, to get the police to step up the hunt. They used a picture of Petra Ware, headlined MOCKED BY MY SON'S KILLER.

Now I'm on the lookout for the K. Everyone is. Most people assume that with the letters still appearing, there will be more murders. I take Paddy with me when I go out. He is used to me now, and he likes the walk. One afternoon, I cut through the cemetery on my way back from town, just wondering if the K is on a gravestone or monument. I am trying to imagine I'm the alphabet writer. Where is the logic? If he's done a church now, then maybe a graveyard next? Besides, Jake and Michelle's ashes are there, spread under the yew trees in the memorial garden. The murder scene itself is the place most people associate with the couple, but the painter has already been there. I figure this might be next.

There is no one around as Paddy leads me down the rows of marble and stone slabs. As we get near to the memorial garden, I can see no scarlet on the headstones, but there is an old coat on the grass under the yew trees. I wonder if it's Jake's? Or Michelle's? Maybe it's a gift from one of their friends, a token to keep them warm in death.

Paddy runs ahead of me and sniffs the coat. He takes it in his teeth and picks it up. The memorial garden is the highest point of the cemetery and I'm scanning the whole place for scarlet. Paddy gives me the coat, so I go to put it straight back. But the coat isn't a gift for the next world. It is doing a job in this one. Michelle's sister Ally is lying on her back on the patch of ground where her sister's ashes are scattered. The coat has been covering her up. Her eyes are closed, and her arms are straight down by her sides. I don't know what to do, so I throw the heavy coat down onto her, to see how she will react. She flinches when it hits her, and opens her eyes.

'Ally?' She looks amazed at the sound of her own name.

'How d'you know it's me? What can you see?'

The dog sniffs around her, but she doesn't move. I ask her if she is hurt. She waves a hand in front of her face.

'The flies are coming for me now.'

'There are no flies.'

'It's a swarm.'

I look around, for someone to help with this conversation, but there's no one else in the cemetery.

'I'm amazed you saw me.'

I'm getting annoyed with this. I tell her that an old coat stands out in a graveyard. She closes her eyes, and repeats her own name three or four times under her breath. I look at my watch and call the dog to heel. Ally opens her eyes, looking at me for the first time. She says she's been waiting for hours, but no one has come to bury her. I point out that they don't usually bury the living. There's a law against it.

'No, no, no . . .' She is wafting away imaginary flies again. 'I've almost gone. My blood's gone, my stomach's gone. They're turning to sand, silt, something like that. They're getting heavy, filling up.'

'Are you ill or something?'

She raises a thin smile, tells me there isn't enough of her left to be ill. She is going. She is almost gone. Across the cemetery, a thin figure in a long waterproof is heading for us. It's Petra Ware. I call the dog, and set off walking in the other direction. At the gate, I turn back and see Petra kneeling by the side of Ally. She is getting things out of a bag.

I wake up with a headache. The night has been very hot and I haven't slept well. I go to the kitchen to get some tablets. I need some juice to wash them down, but all I have is apple juice. I don't like the look of that, so I pour it down the sink and settle for water. I've just got the tablets down when the phone rings. It's Che. He's at work, doing his early morning checks, and he's found a K in the middle of the Bluebird Centre. He thinks it's the K I've been looking for.

I ask him exactly where it is, and he laughs. It's on the inside of the phoney Aztec temple in the jungle in the central atrium. I ask Che how long I've got before the shoppers are let into the Bluebird. He says I've got an hour. I hope the tablets are quick to work. I want a clear head for this one.

I didn't know what to do after photographing the car. I'd finished up the film on my burnt-out Auburn 851, then gone back to my room. I went to bed, although it wasn't bedtime, and I dozed for an hour or so to clear my head. Then I rang the police, and rang my mother. All the way home, my mother was crying, crying for her mother? For herself? For me? I didn't know. I sat in the passenger seat, with my camera on my lap, turning it and polishing its leather case with my sleeve.

Every now and again she would make herself stop crying, and say something. She told me we would be living in a new house, just her and me. She said my room was all ready. She told me how much she'd missed me. She told me how much my grandmother had loved me. I remember at that point looking out of the window, at a field with two horses standing in the rain. Dark grey horses, like statues of themselves.

My mother asked me to choose a present, a welcome-home present. I said I wanted a developing kit to go with my camera. I didn't know what a developing kit was, but I knew I was never going to let anyone else develop this film. If I had a kit, I'd be self-sufficient, I could make my own pictures. She nodded, said something like 'Of course, of course,' but I wondered if she'd heard me. Her mind seemed to be somewhere else. Nonetheless, I got the kit. I turned my bedroom into a darkroom, and that became my refuge. The darkroom became my Auburn 851.

When I get to the Bluebird, Che is waiting at the doors. He ushers me in and we hurry down to the central atrium. I've got used to seeing Che in a white boiler suit, but he looks a lot better as a security guard. In the atrium, he points me towards the plastic jungle, then says he has to go.

I step over the low wall as I've seen Sligo do – repeatedly – on Che's video. I brush past cloth and plastic foliage to get a good view of the Aztec temple. I look around and climb inside. There is no doubt, it's the real K – same red, same style. I'm beginning to recognise the brushwork, like an art historian. I've never seen the painter in action, but I'm the expert on his style. Not just expert, admirer too.

When I've finished with the K, I put the camera in its bag, but I can't leave the temple just yet. I'm inside the head of Adam Sligo, imagining this as his refuge, his hiding-place, imagining him hunkering down for the night with a stolen dinner, and a stolen set of clothes for the next day.

The temple is empty now, with gravel on the floor, and unpainted plastic on the inside of the walls. In the corner is a bucket of sand. It has a cigarette butt in it, and the sand looks as if it was once spread on the floor, since there are traces of sand in the gravel, and gravel in the sand. I pick up the heavy metal bucket, and tip it out. I just want the temple to look more homely, more authentic. I smooth the sand, pick up the cigarette butt, and throw it out into the jungle.

XII

Distortion Series – Image Four: It reminds me of a war zone. It's almost a visual cliché – a bunch of guerrillas, or freedom fighters, or boy soldiers riding through town on the back of a pickup truck, bristling with weapons. Sometimes the bystanders are cheering at the truck, sometimes they're cowering in the shadows. Either way, it's clear who has the power.

It may be a cliché in some places, but it's far from that here. In a small English market town it's weird, unsettling. We've all seen them in the last few weeks. Sometimes they wear masks, sometimes not. They come out at night, and if they have any weapons they keep them out of view.

A couple of times, I've seen them ripping the pictures off advertising hoardings, but mainly I just catch them driving, watching us all. If anyone asks them, they'll tell you how they see their job. They're hunting for Sligo. The police can't catch him, so someone has to take up the challenge. Someone has to safeguard the people of this town.

So they cruise the streets, looking for Adam, looking for newly painted letters. Usually there are three of them in the back, sometimes four. All dressed in white, in a white pickup truck.

*

I owe Che a good turn. Several good turns. Not only did he tip me off about the scarlet K in the Bluebird Centre, not only did he take me to it so I could get a picture, but he even bailed me out when I stayed in there too long. He said I should be in and out of the phoney jungle, in and out of the Aztec temple, within a minute. That was short enough for him to turn a blind eye to the security camera. Twenty minutes, and that starts to look odd.

So after twenty minutes Che came and got me, found me drawing in the sand inside the temple. I'd smoothed out the fire-bucket sand with my hands until it made a thin carpet. Then I sat down in the corner, and wrote the alphabet in the sand with my finger, in a half-moon shape fencing myself in. I got to K and stopped.

Che was furious. I'd promised to be in and out fast. He was annoyed about the sand too. He gathered it up in handfuls and dropped it back into the bucket. His job was on the line now. He said he'd have to ditch the tape. By forcing him to come in and get me, I'd incriminated him and myself. I photographed the scarlet K and left. Che looked flushed. The collar of his uniform dug into his neck.

Morning is the best time to look at the edgelands. Well, morning and evening, after a downpour, when rain puts a sheen on the great metal coils of the power plant, a gloss on the backs of the serried rows of trucks. All the untended clumps of blackberry and hawthorn, wild rose and blackthorn seem to unfurl and flourish, unnoticed by everyone but me.

Yes, most places look their best at the edges of the day, when the sun's low and the whole place is lit like a film set. I can see the appeal of the movies. I can see how Weegee got tempted away from his Speed Graphic Camera – his Aladdin's Lamp – seduced by Hollywood. But he regretted it of course. He lost control.

As a shutterbug, he kept all he needed in the trunk of his Chevy. As a movie director he had teams with him, assistant this and that, chief this and that. He hated it, and I would too. I can come home from a shoot, walk into my darkroom with the picture still vivid and fresh in my mind's eye, then produce that same image on a sheet of paper. It's like printing a memory.

I'm in the habit of an early drive now, since I don't sleep too well, and I always take the camera in case I come across another letter. So I'm doing my morning cruise around the edgelands, heading past the Multiplex Cinema, when I catch sight of some red from the corner of my eye. I'm attuned to it now – the particular shade – I can sort out the salmon pinks from the scarlets without a proper look. I'm locked on in my hunt for the letters, and right outside the Multiplex I'm picking up scarlet. I slow down and study the row of movie posters outside the front door. One of them is selling a remake of *The Exorcist*, there's a picture of a hand holding out a crucifix, and a girl looking terrified. Across the whole image is a thick red L, obscuring the girl's right eye and cutting the crucifix in two.

I'm out taking shots almost before the car's stopped, because I can see another car pulling up outside. He must be a manager here, because he's rushing up holding his hand out, trying to get me to stop. He unlocks the poster box and takes the plastic front off it. For a split second, as he lifts it away, it catches the early morning sun, and I'm not quite quick enough to get a picture of the manager holding a sheet of clear plastic up against the sky, with a scarlet L shot through with light. He rushes inside to clean it off, but I've got what I need.

Letters on church doors, stories about candles and ritual murders, the rumour mill doesn't need much help. Now, with my shots of the L on a poster for *The Exorcist* I know I'm lighting the touch-paper. But it's not my job to worry about that. It's my job to document.

I have no excuse to give to Che. It was simply unprofessional. He tipped me off about the K, gave me a deadline to get in and out, and I missed it. He had to come and fetch me.

I offered to do some portraits for him – by way of an apology – but he wasn't interested. Worst of all, he clammed up. He knew he'd got me hooked, after seeing his video of Sligo's days in the Bluebird Centre, so he'd been passing on more and more detail as he picked it up at work.

On the night they checked the tapes and realised that Sligo had hidden in the phoney jungle, Che and another guard had gone down to see if he'd left any traces. They were under strict instructions not to touch anything they found. That was for the police. The way

Che told the story, his mate went in first and just laughed, calling Che to follow him. It was like a hotel room in there. Not only had Sligo managed to shoplift a range of disguises from the clothes shops, he'd even got a metal rail on wheels to hang up his outfits, so he didn't look dishevelled as he played the part of a casual shopper.

In one corner, a stolen kitchen pedal bin looked out of place in the plastic Aztec temple. Che pressed the pedal. It was half full of empty drinks cans, triangular sandwich packets, even a string net with one shrivelled orange still in it. That really stuck with me. He was eating fruit, looking after himself. What was his vision of the future?

He had a radio, stolen again, tuned to a music station. I talked about that with Che. Music might help take his mind off things, but if I was him I'd be tuned to the police channels, to see if they were closing in. Not if he didn't do it. That was Che's point. Not if he was innocent. I don't buy that. If he was innocent, why was he hiding in a plastic jungle?

Apart from the food and clothes, they found two camping stools and a sleeping bag. The bag looked like he'd brought it with him. It was old and threadbare, but the stools were new, lifted from the camping shop. Why two stools? Che had thought about that. He said you have to imagine Sligo holed up in the temple hour on hour, slipping out in different guises only when he needed something. The two stools were to stop him going mad. That was Che's theory. He could pretend he wasn't alone, pretend someone else was just on their way over. I said if that wasn't madness, I didn't know what was.

It's a buzz, no question. I should have shaken that Multiplex manager by the hand when he took the poster box down. I got my shots, and he made sure they were exclusive. Thank you, and have a nice day. Not only could no one else photograph the L, no one else would see it until my pictures hit the newspapers. Worth raising my fee I think, worth asking Alex for a bonus.

I get the prints pegged up to dry and head out of the darkroom. It's barely breakfast time and I've already shot the L and printed it. It's too early to ring Alex and I don't talk to anyone else on that paper, so I head for the coffee.

I've left my front door ajar, hoping that Paddy will come and see me. But when the door opens, it's not a dog who comes in. It's a guy of about fifty, in a crumpled suit and tie, with a fedora and an overcoat. He's balding, unshaven. For a moment, I think I've lost the plot. It's Weegee come to haunt me, come to punish me for giving up the radios. He coughs. He speaks. It's not Weegee, at least not quite. There is an American accent there, but it's soft and southern, not New York. I assume he's a new member of the group, a new convert for Calladine, too new to know about the white clothes rule. I reach past him for the coffee.

'You come to see Calladine?'

'No, Perry Scholes.'

'Right. Yes, I'm waiting for Perry too. Why d'you want him?'

He smiles and holds out a hand. I own up.

Turns out he doesn't know Calladine. He came to see me. Says it's personal and business. He ushers me into my own living room and shuts the front door.

I offer him coffee, to try to regain a bit of control. It's my flat, and I'm playing host here. He follows me back into the kitchen.

'I'll get to the point . . .' He's pulling the kitchen door shut behind him. I'm starting to feel claustrophobic here.

'Names first. You know my name, but you didn't introduce yourself . . .'

'Arthur.'

Arthur. Arthur was Weegee's real name. He looks like him and he shares a first name. But Weegee's dead and buried, and this man doesn't sound like a New Yorker, and why would the ghost of Weegee haunt me in my kitchen?

'Arthur James. Does the surname mean anything to you?' It doesn't. And it's not Weegee's either. I'm shaking my head and measuring out the coffee.

'I'm Michelle's father. You know, the girl . . .'

strange to call him grandfather without ever meeting him – spent the first years of their married life in Hong Kong. He worked for the police out there. High up. Desk job.

He had a brilliant young detective – local, knew all the alleys and dens – who was on the verge of cracking a gang. Prostitution, drugs, the lot, but gambling was their main business. So this detective goes undercover for months, deep cover, in up to his eyes. He's getting great stuff, paperwork, tapes, almost enough to nail them. Then he vanishes.

They wait for him, his bosses at the station. They wait and wait, but they hear nothing. So they send in another guy – undercover again – and he comes out a few days later like he's seen a ghost. They get him back to the station, feed him coffee, sit him down. What happened to the brilliant young detective? Was his cover blown? Did they shoot him? Worse than that.

The story was that he'd been playing on the tables to maintain his cover, playing a couple of times a week for a while, when a terrible thing happened – he started winning. He won twice in one weekend, not much because his stake was small, but he was winning nonetheless. Next weekend he doubled his stake, played once, won again. His luck was in.

That detective had been brought up to trust in the magical power of luck. He believed that every man gets one good run. Just one. When you get it, you have to ride it, because it's the only chance you'll get to live a charmed life. So when his number comes up on the tables for the third time in a row, and the croupiers are gritting their teeth at him, and the heavies

125

are cracking their knuckles in the background, what does he do? He's an undercover cop and he's drawing attention to himself. He should stop gambling. But if this is his one run of luck, then only a fool would pass it up.

Within days of the third win, he's sold his apartment, and his mother's apartment, and checked them both into a hotel. Next weekend, he walks into a rival casino and slaps the whole lot on number 3.

I admire that kind of risk-taking. My grandmother didn't. She called it plain stupid, and told it as a cautionary tale. But that made me admire it even more. When she moved in for the punchline, lowering her voice to tell me how the ball hovered on the edge of 3, then skittered out, I knew she wanted me to gasp, to shake my head. But I didn't feel like that. I didn't think it mattered what the number was.

Even when she told me that they'd found his body, bloated after days in the sea, I still applauded him for taking the chance. Apparently, they found his mother still in the hotel room, waiting for him. She'd been living on room service, and he'd left enough cash at the hotel to cover her bill. It was my grandfather's job to go round and break the news. When he told her, she looked desperate for a moment, as if she was going to collapse, then she shrugged and said, 'So it wasn't his lucky streak. I told him to test it first.'

It took me a while to get rid of Arthur James. He was persistent. Charming enough, but persistent. He'd been asking around. My name had come up as the last person to see his daughter alive. He'd heard about her last words, or last word. He'd heard that I might have pictures of his daughter's final moments and he wanted to see them. I tried to tell him that she was dead when I got there, but he thought I was trying to shield him from her final desperate moments.

'Petra's told me all about it.'

'I told her I don't have pictures.'

'Petra thinks you do.'

I shrugged. I was sipping my coffee, trying not to meet his eyes. He was locked on, staring at me. I was cornered in my own kitchen.

'I want to see them. Do you have kids, Perry?'

I shook my head.

'I live an ocean away. I don't see much of Ally and Michelle now.' Saying her name, and using it in the present tense, pulled him up short. He rubbed his face with his hands for a moment and I slid past him. I made my apologies, put my coat on, and left. I drove around for half an hour and when I got back he had gone. I don't know if he'd tried the darkroom door, but the lock was still fast. He'd left no note in the flat. My print of *Napalm* – the Vietnam shot – was back up. I'd left it propped behind a sofa with its face to the wall, ever since Calladine attacked me for it.

As ever, work was the answer, even when I didn't know the question. I had no new letters to print up, no sign of an M. But I had some still-life shots I'd not developed, so I started on them. I did them quickly, hung them up to dry, then lifted the floorboard and got out the Untaken Photographs. What good would these do for a father? There were close-ups of Jake, and wide shots of both, but Michelle's close-ups had rattled me, and I'd let them run to black. Why would he want to see these? Even in the wide shots, you can see the huge dark stain on her summer shirt where her chest broke open. You can see her head, propped against Jake's shoulder, and a dribble of blood from her mouth onto his shirt.

Maybe TJ was right. I'd kept the gun locked in the darkroom, but after the M appeared I started carrying it round with me. A church door was one thing, but an altar, well, that tipped it over the edge. The priest had called the paper first, and Alex called me. He'd asked the priest to give us half an hour before calling the police.

It was a plain, modern, brick church in the edge-lands, between Mister Motor's yard and the Bluebird Centre. The lock had been forced with something like a crowbar and a huge M was emblazoned on the altar. It was unmistakeable, to me anyway. It was the real thing. It wasn't the M that shocked me. That was as well made as ever. It was long and flat to fit the shape of the altar, and it was weighted to perfection, standing out against the white stone. How could an artist who took such trouble with the geometry of an M leave such a trail of devastation elsewhere in the church?

The tiled floor was strewn with bits of coloured plaster from broken statues. Some pieces were powdered, as if ground in with a heel. The priest was on his hands and knees, muttering prayers under his breath as he gathered up the crumbs of wafer from the floor behind the altar. It looked as though these had been ground in with a heel too, but the priest was eating them, eating and praying.

I took my pictures of the M and sat down. I felt like I should say a prayer too. But I couldn't think of anything to say, so I left. At the door, I turned and took one wide shot of the desecrated church.

Once the paper ran those pictures, the mood in the town changed. There were rumours of satanic symbols being found in the church, but I didn't see any. Nonetheless, I knew I wouldn't see any more fake letters, or ADAM on the back of football shirts. When I drove around the place, people stared at me. Not just at me, but at every car, and at each other. Everyone was looking out for Sligo. I saw a shopkeeper near the church boarding up his windows. I heard another shopkeeper browbeating him for giving in to fear. I saw – as I drew up alongside – two children lying flat and scared across the back seat of a car. I saw school-yards empty at playtime, and pubs full at closing time. I saw the town close in upon itself.

There were more police on the streets, and more rumoured sightings of the killer. I wondered if the letters would stop there – halfway through the alphabet. Wherever he was, Adam Sligo must be living in fear now. Anyone caught in the act, or caught with a tin of scarlet paint for that matter, ran the risk of being lynched.

XIV

Even now I prefer monochrome to colour. On rare occasions, I'll use colour film, because the websites like it, the magazines like it. But it's fundamentally phoney. Black and white means light and shade. It's ancient, somehow organic. With colour, some manufacturer has made a choice – how red will the reds be, how warm? I can tell an Agfa red from a Fuji red from a Kodak red.

Not only that, I can tell a 1950s red from a 60s red; and they're all on the wane now. In boxes, albums and frames across the world, the captured past is getting paler and paler. The blood is draining from the faces of our parents, our grandparents; and in a hundred years they will be blank. Not the black and white shots though, we'll still have those, chiselled out of light as tough as stone.

Despite all her coaching, all those weeks of learning not to trust, I knew that my first film had worked. I know plenty of shutterbugs who can't breathe until it's out on the paper in front of them – until it's printed, it doesn't exist. When I got back to my mum's house, I wrapped my camera in a handkerchief, and put it the back of a drawer.

To my surprise, she gave me my developing kit that same week, but I was in no rush. I knew it was all there, safe and warm inside its box. I took my time, read the beginner's guide she bought me, laid out the trays, the measuring jugs, the concertina bottles of chemicals. Then one afternoon – late, not too bright – I told my mum the bedroom was off-limits until I came out.

I taped sheets of card to the window, then taped around the edges, where the light was leaking in. Then I drew the curtains. I taped around the doorframe and stood in the middle of the room, straining to detect any trace of light. I taped the keyhole, and stood in the echoing, absolute darkness. My bedroom was light-tight. Finally I switched on the red safe-light and began to work.

In those hours of alchemy, I conjured the house, the dog, the car. But best of all I conjured my grandmother, returned to calm, returned almost to beauty. She was at one with the water, fully clothed and lifeless, drowned in her own pond.

I don't know if she'd rescued the dog, or if the dog had rescued itself, but in the pictures, he'd shaken himself dry and looked the same as ever. He was sitting by the edge of the pond, waiting for her to climb out. Of course, when I went downstairs to show my mum the first fruits of my camera, I had to be selective. I showed her the dog by the pond, the car in the woods, my bedroom. Nothing from the last day. She asked me why there weren't any shots of my grandmother, after all the weeks I'd spent there. I told her I had taken some, but they were over-exposed.

*

It was the biggest letter yet. Not the best painted though. For a few minutes, I stood with the camera in my hand and weighed up if it was a fake. But no. There were no fakes any more, the stakes were much too high. And besides, it was exactly the right colour, and well enough made to be authentic. I put its slight imperfections down to the technical difficulty – the side of the edgelands gasometer was huge, rusted and curved. I took it good and wide, to show the context – shrine, vision, the whole landscape.

I hadn't heard about the N until I was tipped off by TJ. He came to my flat to give me the news. He was armed, as always, close to the edge, but there was a note of triumph in his voice.

'I warned you. I've been warning everyone. Those satanic letters haven't stopped.'

I sat down and offered him a chair. He leaned back in it, but winced and lurched forward.

'What's wrong? Are you in pain?'

He turned his back on me and lifted up his shirt. There were two long cuts in his back, one vertical, one horizontal, in the shape of a cross. They looked raw, partly scabbed, but nowhere near healed. I told him to put his shirt back down, which he did with great care.

'Who did that?'

'Martyn.'

'Why?'

'For protection, of course.'

'Why do you have so many radios?'

It's not a question I welcome.

'I needed all the radios for my work, but I don't do that work any more.'

I still think he looks like Weegee, sympathetic, so I tell him a bit more than I tell most. I even give him the bit about the motorways, about losing my stomach. But he's not listening.

'Where's your Nick Ut print?'

'I took it down again. It seems to worry people.'

'What?' He shook his head, looked behind the sofa, found the Vietnam shot and hung it back on the wall. He knows the name of the photographer. That's special. Perhaps he is the ghost of Weegee, son of Weegee, Weegee's representative on earth. With the back of his finger, he strokes the image of the naked girl running down the street towards us. It makes me feel uncomfortable.

'You know what happened after this shot was taken?'

I do. So I tell him. 'She's married, with kids, living in Canada.'

'No, I mean just after.'

'Dunno. Someone must have got her some treatment.'

'Not someone. It was Nick.' He turns and points at me. 'The guy with the camera.'

'Really?'

'She's running to Nick shouting "Too hot! Too hot!" and when she reaches him, she faints in his arms. He rushes her to hospital in Saigon – in his car – and she spends a year there, graft after graft.'

'So he saved her?'

'He saved her, and he got the shot. Which was more important, Perry?'

I don't like being tricked, and I feel I'm being tricked. I tell him nothing justifies the shot. Save the girl, that's all. That's what seems right just now, so that's what I tell Arthur. That's what I say to the American. To Weegee. But he looks crestfallen, shakes his head. I start making coffee, and he follows me into the kitchen. I try a change of tack.

'Do you know any more of Nick Ut's work?'

'Nothing.' He looks sheepish. 'It's not the kind of work I can sell.'

'Sorry?'

'I run a gallery.'

I'm getting excited now. I'm wondering whether to get out my still-life portfolio. But he can see what I'm thinking.

'Not a photographic gallery, I'm afraid.'

'No?'

'No. I wish. It's watercolours, seascapes. If they're not sun-drenched with boats in them, the tourists won't buy, so Nick's well beyond the pale.'

'You call him Nick, like you know him.'

'He meant a lot to a friend of mine.'

I pour two coffees, hand him one, and go back in my living room. This time, I take the best chair, and he sits across from me. I feel the need to remind him who's host here.

'What do you want from me, Arthur?'

'You know what I want.'

'I don't have the shots.'

'Any photographer would keep the negs at least. You were there, at the murder scene?'

I don't like this feeling. It's early morning, and I'm

being nailed to my chair by a man who wants my Untaken Photos.

Distortion Series – Image Five: It's Chinese whispers. Every time I hear the story, the details are different. What's clear is this much: there's an abandoned concrete ammunition bunker round the back of the allotments, in the edgelands. One morning, its gun slots and arched doorway were boarded up. Everything else is speculation.

Did someone find a stash of red paint in among the lager cans, fag ends, needles? On summer days, the stench of urine drifted from the bunker out across the allotments. I'm glad to see the thing boarded up, paint or no paint. Was Sligo hiding in there? Sometimes I wonder if they'll ever catch him.

Some say they saw men in white overalls doing the boarding up. Will it stop the alphabet? It's not hard to get hold of more scarlet paint. I'm still on the lookout for an O.

XV

The storks were still there, but the trees had gone. The whole forest had vanished. I wasn't surprised by this. The river now ran through the middle of the edgelands, roughly following the course of the main road. The storks were lining the edges of every roof, every wall. They were silent but menacing, like a grotesque parody of swallows in migration lines, a scene from Hitchcock's *The Birds*.

As before, the boat put in at a small inlet, still an Ashanti village, but now located in the square where Jake and Michelle were murdered. Children ran and played between the huts, smoke curled from fires between them. On the edge of the village, I could see as the boat got closer the rusted shell of Jake's old BMW. Though there were no trees, there were tall grasses and low bushes, and the car was almost camouflaged.

For some reason, the boat couldn't stop, so as it slowed beside the village we had to jump from the deck onto the riverbank. I watched my fellow passengers make the leap, landing on all fours, or staggering to keep their balance, brushing off their white suits and long cotton dresses as they found their feet. I kicked off hard from the edge of the deck and cleared the shallows. Those who had made the jump before me were pulling out cameras, eager to record the village ritual.

This time, I knew it was a kind of funeral. I knew it was a baby wrapped in all that foliage. Even so, I felt I had to join the line, to play my part. I took my place down at the edge of the river. My chestnut brogues were sinking in the shale and the water was lapping at the leather. In the background I could hear the sound of heavy breathing – deep and slow. I looked around and saw the gasometer – emblazoned with an N – rising and falling, expanding and contracting like an iron lung, and I realised that the gas it held was air. It didn't store air, it made it, then pushed it out for us to breathe.

After what seemed like hours, the bundle of leaves was passed to me. As before, I knew I was expected to kiss the child, to kiss her then gently lay her in the lap of the river. I looked down, the face was tiny, eyes dead but open. I didn't want to kiss her, but I did it, then I reached down and set her on the water.

The bundle turned in the current, but wasn't swept downstream. The pull was strong. I could see the water plaiting and knotting as it swept out of the edgelands into open country. Yet the baby turned, slowly once around, then began to sink. Some of the village elders waded in to try to grab her, but she went too fast. Within seconds she was gone, and though we stared downstream for ages after, she never broke the surface again.

I wake up, and it's far from morning. A sharp wind is rising and falling against the windows. The dream itself was not unsettling. In fact, as I watched the dead child swallowed by the river, it felt right, like a burial. But now I can't get back to sleep. My mind is locked on the face of the baby. If I shut my eyes, her eyes are staring back at me. I sit up, tilt the blind and look out of the window. The moon is full. I can see the edge-lands ghosted with its light. Through the middle, through the heart, sweeps a road that shines like a river.

Now I can see what they are up to, this cult across the corridor. They sent Che to befriend me. But I got Che into trouble at the Bluebird, and now he won't give me the time of day. So they sent TJ to cosy up to me instead. That's fine. As long as I know. I'm not going to turn TJ away, because that would make them think they're getting to me. I'll keep on friendly terms, but from now on, my guard's up.

'I tell you, that woman is paranoid.'

So says the man in camouflage trousers, jacket and cap, stripping down and cleaning his gun on my living-room floor.

'I guess she could say the same about you.' I nod at the weapon in pieces on my carpet. TJ looks me up and down, baffled, and gets back to the ritual of wiping, blowing, polishing. Compared with TJ's armoury, Petra Ware's gesture seems mild.

TJ's gun is reassembled. He points it at my face.

'Get it away!'

'Not loaded.'

'I don't care. Don't point it here.'

'You think I'm paranoid?'

'A bit.'

He looks annoyed, then worried. He makes me fetch the gun he gave me, to check I've kept it clean and close at hand.

'He'll come for us, Perry. It's not paranoia, just fact.'

'Who?'

'Sligo.'

I feel the need to change the subject.

'This barrier Petra's painted. Where does it run?'

'Round the murder scene. About six feet away. Now that's paranoia. What's it for? Who's she scared of?'

'How do you know it's meant to keep people out, TJ? If she wanted to do that, why didn't she put up a wall?'

'Maybe she doesn't know any bricklayers. Paint's cheaper.'

'Right round, you say?'

'Right round that heap of flowers and toys, yeah.'

'What colour paint?'

He looks around the room, and points at a football scarf draped over the back of a dining chair. I've taken to wearing it on cooler evenings, as a way of standing out from the white suits across the corridor. It's hard to miss – long and broad, and brightest scarlet.

It must have been the late 1970s. Arthur didn't say, but I did the sums in my head. He was living in Florida, making a packet selling sunny pictures to tourists, but, like a lot of expats, he had the odd sad night when he needed a piece of home. So he drove the twenty miles or so to Disney World of all places.

He'd been there with his daughters, so he knew his way around. He skipped the Magic Kingdom – not interested in men dressed up as mice – and headed for the International Village.

It was like a massive food hall on the edge of an artificial lake. You could eat pasta in a scaled-down replica of St Mark's Square in Venice, then slip down an alley and come out in Beijing. So Arthur crossed Italy, China, France, India, until he reached a dimly lit village green. There was a red pillar box and a gaslight glow from inside the houses. A Victorian policeman paced out his beat, bidding goodnight to passers-by in a bad cockney accent.

Inside the Queen's Arms, there was a phoney fire in the grate, and imported beer in the pumps, but it was a taste of England all the same. Arthur pulled up a stool, sat at the bar, and ordered a pint.

On one side of him he could hear two expat English businessmen discussing how much money they were making, how glad they were that they had left the sad old homeland. So glad that they came to a fake London pub to congratulate themselves.

On the other side, there was a guy on his own, so Arthur struck up a conversation. He was not an Englishman, to Arthur's relief. He introduced himself as Tom, said he'd got some heavy personal stuff going on, so he'd come here for a change of scene. He'd had some green tea in the Forbidden City, a pizza in St Mark's Square, and now he'd come for a pint of warm, dark English beer at the Queen's Arms.

They talked about the usual stuff – the heat, the tourists, the crime – then Tom took out his wallet, and Arthur thought he was going to buy another beer. Instead, he pulled out a folded cutting from a newspaper, and spread it on the bar in front of them.

It was Nick Ut's *Napalm*, on the front page of the *Washington Post*. Of course, Arthur had seen it before, it had been around for years, won the Pulitzer Prize no less. But Tom was obsessed with it, knew all the details. He told Arthur the whole story. There was a mother with seven kids in a village called Trang Bang north of Saigon. She was trying to protect her kids from the fighting, so they were holed up in a temple, thinking it would be the safest place. Then the air-raid siren went off next to them and she panicked. She shouted to her kids, 'Get out! Run down the road! Run down the main road!' So that's what they did.

The road was known as Route One. Captain Thomas J Kelly was in the line of command that gave the order to bomb Route One, and now he was sitting on a bar stool in Disney World pouring out his heart to a stranger.

'You wanna know the punchline?' Arthur waits for my answer. It's the third morning in a week he's turned up in my flat. I'm getting used to him. He knows his way around photography, and I like talking to people who know their way around photography.

'Okay, what's the punchline?' It strikes me as an odd phrase. Maybe this is going to wind up as a joke, but I can't see it.

'Well, I never saw Tom Kelly again after that night, but I read in the papers a year or so later, he'd become some kind of therapist or something.' If it's a joke, I don't get it.

'That's the punchline?'

He nods. 'Nick Ut could have responded like a civilised human being, dropped the camera and focused everything on helping the girl. But he took the shot. He took it, and he sent it into the world. Because of that, the anti-war protesters had their defining image, and the guy in charge of the napalm spent the rest of his life in penitence. All because that picture drilled into his brain. It wouldn't let him go.'

My copy of *Napalm* is back on the wall, thanks to Arthur. He's right. That picture made a difference. I'm not going to let myself be shamed into hiding it again. I'm staring at the picture, but Arthur is fixed on me. I can feel it. I don't meet his eye, because I know what he's going to say.

The original Arthur – Mr Fellig – was an artist first and foremost. Some of his shots may have pricked a conscience, helped to change a New York law or two, but most of them were just done for the beauty.

As I'm unlocking the darkroom door, scarcely believing that I'm going to show Michelle's father my shots of his dead daughter, he's jabbering on about war photography. I'm not listening. In my mind's eye there's a Weegee classic – *Dead Boccia Player*. Story was that a group of mobsters – not big guns, but hangers-on – are in a game of Italian bowls, and it's a close match. So close, in fact, that a tailor's tape measure can't produce a winner. There's an argument, then a fist fight, then a gun is pulled and suddenly there's a loser.

Weegee picks it up on his radio, speeds round to the park, and gets there first – as ever. I can imagine the scene as he arrives – the other players screaming and fighting – holding down the guy who pulled the gun, waiting for the sirens. Instead, along comes a shutterbug, and he starts framing up on the loser's corpse.

Framing up. That's the key. That's the genius. He doesn't just point and shoot. I've studied that picture time and time again. He must have walked around the body, chosen his angle with the face tipped away from the shot. Now, that wasn't out of sympathy for the family. Lots of Weegee shots are full face. That angle was because with the face away he could crouch and frame up on the other side of a metal bucket full of bowls to give some foreground, and he could get the cap in shot, the victim's cloth cap, which lies a foot away from the top of his head.

If you stare at him for long enough, the corpse begins to float. His arms are by his sides, his ankles crossed. He looks like a laid-back magician floating above a bucket of bowls. The longer you look, the more weightless he becomes.

Did Weegee move the bucket an inch or two, so it was perfect? Did he kick the cap a little closer to its owner, so it made it into shot? I like to think so. I like to think his attention to detail, his quest for the perfect shot, would let him do that.

I wish I'd spent a little more time arranging Jake and Michelle. I should have taken her off his shoulder, turned her face round a bit. But I didn't have the time. Weegee always had the time.

'Before you see these, I want to remind you that I

didn't offer to show you. You asked. I didn't want to get them out.' Arthur nods. 'Of course, of course.' But his eyes are fixed on my hands, carrying the box of Untaken Photographs out of my darkroom.

When he sees the first wide shot, of the two victims framed by the windscreen, he takes it from me gently, and looks hard and close. His face is set, but I catch a trace of something in his eyes.

I try to take the picture back from him. 'You don't have to see any more.' I say. 'I don't have any close-ups of her. Just wides.'

'I'd like to see them anyway, please.' His eyes are already on the next shot in the pile. I hand it over.

'Why are you doing this to yourself?' I wait, but he doesn't reply. He just keeps staring at the pictures. I don't like this at all. I've been presenting the living with pictures of their dead all my career, but there's usually a newspaper between us. It doesn't feel right to be doing it one to one.

We look at the last picture in silence, then he pockets the prints and walks straight to the window. He throws it open, and for a second I think he's going to jump, but he leans on the sill and takes some deep breaths. Then he wipes his face with a handkerchief. I'm glad I destroyed the big close-ups of Michelle. He buttons his jacket, and walks out without saying a word.

Things have gone quiet across the corridor. Calladine seems to have gone away. For good, I hope. Some of his people still turn up, but they don't stay long. I get the impression they don't know where he is, or when he's coming back. I feel sorry for the dog, and I wonder if he's getting fed. I stand out in the corridor and call him, but there's no response.

His front door's ajar, so I push it and peer inside, calling for Paddy. The dog's there, looking sleepy and well-fed, but he's not alone. The smart-looking woman is there in a chair by the window. I wonder if I should say sorry for tipping whisky on her last time we met, but I decide against it.

'He's been away for days. No one knows where,' she says.

She takes a drag on a cigarette, but she's not a smoker, and she chokes on it. She's got a full tumbler of whisky on the arm of her chair.

'Just looking for the dog actually.'

She lifts up the bottle, offering me a drink. I shake my head.

'It's nine in the morning.'

'He who tries to save his life will lose it . . .' She points a finger as she speaks. I tell her I have to get to work. I look at Paddy, hoping he'll follow me out, but he stays where he is.

When I get to the murder scene, there's a couple of curious office workers looking at the painted line around it. My problem is how to get a shot of the O looking like an O. I park the car, hide the camera under my coat and duck into the HQ of Collegiate Insurance. I ask for the claims department, hoping it's in the penthouse, and the lady says go in the lift to the second-floor reception. I get my visitor's pass, call a lift, and press button 8.

The top floor of the Collegiate Tower is a canteen.

I buy a coffee to look natural, get a window table, and look down. It's good. The O is a little broken by some bouquets of flowers, but it's clear enough. It's break time, and the clerks are coming up in groups. I have to stand, but I hide the camera in my coat and take a few. By the time I'm getting stared at, I've got enough. I swig the coffee, burn my tongue, and leave. I don't blame them for staring. I'd stare too, if I was them. I could be anyone. I could be Adam Sligo. I could have gunned them all down in their own canteen. The company should tighten its security, things being what they are.

When I step into the square again, Petra Ware is standing inside the O, rearranging the flowers for her dead son. She looks dishevelled, like she's just woken up. I keep the camera buttoned inside my coat, but she's not fooled. I can feel her eyes on me all the way over to the car. What does the placing of the O mean? Why would Sligo risk coming back to the murder scene?

As I cross the motorway bridge on my way back from the edgelands, I glance down at the shining streams of colour, and I want to go down there. I want to park the car and take my camera down there. Arthur was right. Taking pictures – whatever the subject – is a noble art. If I belong anywhere, it's down there among the massive, shifting population of the motor-ways. Besides, needs must. Someone's got to give me my daily bread. I resolve to re-tune a radio or two when I get home. I never liked the music channels anyway. Give me the music of police short wave, the drama of life twisting in your hand as you try to keep a hold of it.

XVI

Motorways are a great mystery. You're together and alone at the same time. Sometimes, you are so close to your neighbour you could brush fingertips, but you don't. You dare not. It's the closest to an afterlife I've seen in this one, a serene, seemingly endless drift of humanity – kids waving or picking off drivers with finger-guns, passengers dozing with feet on the dashboard, drivers in trances. We are in communion. We share a common direction, common purpose. But we are untouchable. Souls with no bodies.

Sometimes, the urge to shut my eyes and take my hands off the wheel is hard to resist. A pile-up breaks the trance. Suddenly there are bodies – battered and bleeding perhaps – but real flesh and blood. Instantly, the flow stops, the spell is broken.

Night three, and no RTAs. Nothing at all. I've had the radios on, but it's minor stuff – thefts, brawls, domestics. So I go out hunting. I'm up and down the motorway. My camera is my passenger. The flow is smooth. Once or twice it slows a little and I wonder what's ahead. My shutter finger starts to twitch. Then the flow speeds up again, so I keep driving.

I float alongside a green estate car, packed up for a holiday. The mother is driving, lost in a world of her own. The father is hunched on his side, like he's in bed, eyes shut and mouth open, facing me. In the back, there's a baby cradled in a child seat, swaddled in a sheet and fast asleep. Next to the baby is a girl of maybe six or seven, hugging a doll cheek to cheek, but looking out the window on the other side from me. Her face is turned away, so I can't tell if she's sleeping, or watching the stream of white lights across the central reservation.

I ride more or less level with the holiday family for a while. The father's eyes open as I watch him, and we stare at each other for a moment, then he turns over to sleep facing his wife. If the trance broke now, if a tyre blew, or a driver nodded off, I picture him trapped in the metal, snapped by his seatbelt. I can picture the children too. I've seen it enough times. Sometimes in the past, I've taken comfort in the death of the parents, so at least they won't see what became of their kids.

Could I take it? If it happened, and I got out alive, could I take the pictures? I lost my stomach for the motorway work and I want to be cured. It feels good to be on the road again, but until the moment comes, I can't be sure that I've got my stomach back.

I keep rehearsing details. How blood really is thicker than water, as it rests in a curved pool on the road, with a dark skin holding its shape. How a face turns to plastic as the flesh hardens after death. I remember a man's arm on the hard shoulder, with a woman's name tattooed on it. I recall a lot of eyes, the endless surprise that people die with their eyes open unless somebody shuts them.

Even the master must have worried about losing his stomach. Why else would he use those names? Any new guys on the New York picture desks had to learn Weegee slang so they were ready when he called. For him, a corpse was not a corpse. It was a dry diver if it jumped from a roof or a window. If it was dredged up from the harbour, or washed onto the stones along the coast it was a bottom-feeder. Roasts were the fire victims.

The father in the packed estate car turns to me again, unable to get comfortable. He opens his eyes, but this time he frowns, sits up, says something to his wife, who glances across at me. I ease off the pedal, and my car slips out of sync with theirs. If Weegee found them, and their kids, in a pile of petrol-spattered metal, what name would he give them to protect himself? I think about it all the way home, but I can't come up with anything. When I get home, I unplug the radios I'd left on.

Since me and Jesus got married,
We haven't been a minute apart,
He placed a receiver in my hands,
Religion in my heart,
And I can ring him up easy,
O, I can ring up my Jesus,
Because Jesus gonna make up my dying bed,
Yes, Jesus gonna make up my dying bed.

Ever since he's come back, Calladine's been playing the same song over and over. Worse than that, he's been singing along. Because he never shuts his door,

I've had to put up with it day and night, the same tortured gravel voice and moaning slide guitar.

It's playing this morning when TJ shows up. He wants to talk. He has a new theory about the letters. He thinks he's getting inside Sligo's head, says he's been studying maps, thinks he can predict where the next letter's coming.

I can't stand the music, so I suggest we head out with Paddy for some air. TJ goes across to get the dog. I grab a raincoat from the back of my door, hoping to persuade him to cover up his white kit for a while. He's given up the camouflage, now he looks like all the others.

As we get out onto the road, some blue lights flash past, heading for the motorway.

'You don't have to follow them, you know.' He points at the ambulance.

'I don't follow, I get there first. Anyway, I've given that up.'

'So why were your radios back on the other night?'

'Just listening.'

He pulls a wad of notes out of his pocket, bundled tight with an elastic band. The note on the outside is a twenty. 'Martyn wanted you to have this.'

'No way. I'm not taking his money. Is he buying followers now?'

'It's not like that, Perry.' He pockets the cash.

'Just tell him never to try to bribe me again, TJ. You hear?'

'I hear, but it's not like that.'

We turn into the park to let Paddy have a run. As we pass the church door – now scrubbed and varnished to remove any trace of scarlet – TJ starts talking about the letters again. He tells me to keep an eye on the Soccerdome, or the allotments, or the Territorial Army barracks. He says he thinks the killer is marking out the shape of a question mark across the town.

'Why would he do that?'

'To keep us guessing.'

We have the park to ourselves. With the whole town on killer alert, public spaces are private for anyone who still visits them. Paddy dashes off into the bushes and comes back with something in his mouth. He drops it in my lap, and backs away, head down, tail up, wanting me to throw it for him.

'Ugh! Look at that!' I throw it as far as I can, but he brings it straight back. In my lap again, its eyelids slowly close. I pick it up and throw it. TJ must have seen my face, because he stops talking about the alphabet.

'What's wrong? It's an old doll.'

He goes back to the alphabet, but I'm not listening. The dog is fetching that face again and again, dropping it in my lap. Eventually, TJ tells Paddy to leave us, and he runs off with it.

'Perry, what's your biggest secret?'

'I don't know. What's yours?'

'Well, we're not supposed to tell anyone outside the movement . . .'

So he tells me that the smartly dressed woman I saw in Calladine's flat works at the hospital where they did the post-mortem on Jake and Michelle. She swore the group to secrecy when she told them, but now TJ is telling me.

'She won't keep her job long if she goes round blabbing about it.'

'It's not like that. She told us, so that we could pray for it.'

'For what?'

'For the baby.' I looked blank. 'For Michelle's baby.'

'Michelle didn't have a baby.'

'Yes she did. About ten weeks old. They found it inside her when they cut her body open.'

I don't know what to say. I look into the distance, hoping that Paddy will run back to break the mood. I feel I've been told something I have no right to know. TJ has no right to know it either. If it's true, that is.

I knew Che was pushing his luck, but I still felt guilty when they sacked him for tampering with tapes. He'd run me off a copy of the Sligo tape at work, then one for TJ, and that was just the start. It was a cottage industry. Maybe if I'd been quicker with my pictures of the K, he could have kept out of trouble for longer, but he was always riding for a fall.

When I passed him in the corridor, he blanked me. One morning I got up to find his security-guard uniform crumpled outside my front door.

None of this detracted from the video. The more I watched it, the better it got. Once I had picked Sligo out among the shoppers in each scene, I didn't have to waste time hunting him. After each cut, as a new shop opened up, I could study his panache, his self-sufficiency. He even changed his walk to suit the clothes he'd stolen.

At night, he got changed in the privacy of his Aztec temple. In the daytime, he used the multi-faith prayer room. It had no camera, and was always empty, so the video had clips of him marching in tweed-suited, and strolling out track-suited with the tweeds in a bag. What was not on the tape was any evidence of stealing. In the days he spent at the Bluebird Centre, he stole clothes, food, cigarettes, but none of it on camera.

Just once, I caught him glancing at me through the video. It was in the early hours, and I couldn't sleep. I felt feverish, as if I was going down with something.

I thought of having a drink to settle me, but I didn't think it would help. I put the video on, and sat down with a glass of water. I was feeling drowsy by the end, as I waited for the final scene – my favourite – where Sligo walks calmly through the automatic doors into the open.

That scene always got me, because I knew he must have gone from there straight to Mister Motor's yard, to look for a car like his mother's. Or he walked straight out to start planning his alphabet. I'd rewound and replayed those last frames over and over, as the doors slid open and he sauntered out to cast his spell on the town.

But this time, I didn't reach the departure. I was watching the scene before it when I noticed something for the first time. It was a short clip, and not specially interesting at first glance. It opened with a toyshop – baby and toddler toys, wooden trains and plastic drums. Our camera was pointing at the door. In walked Sligo in a padded coat and woollen hat, looking like he'd just stepped off a ski slope. He stopped in the middle of the shop, scanned quickly left and right to take it in, then turned round and walked out. But before he turned, he looked at me.

Once I'd seen it, I couldn't think how I'd missed it before. I edged back, frame by frame, until I was locked on the moment. We stared at each other. I don't know how long, then I hit PLAY. His shoulders loosened, he turned on his heel and left the shop.

XVII

The old man is a wreck, shivering and barely able to speak. I sit him down in the armchair by my window, where the light is good, and set up the camera. I like portraits, but I don't often do them these days. Most of my subjects are dead. TJ didn't do much to calm him down, just delivered him to me, told me his name, and left. The old man is gibbering and won't sit still. I try to reassure him.

'It's okay. It'll wash off.'

'Dead! He got me! I'm dead!'

'Nobody's got you, George. You'll be fine.' I say I'll get him a drink, but first I step back a few paces and take some shots. When I've got what I need, I lead him to the bathroom sink to wash.

TJ was on patrol first thing this morning, scouting round the town centre looking for a killer. He was cruising down High Street, when this vagrant came staggering towards him down the middle of the road. At first, TJ thought it was a mugging. After all, it looked like blood on the old man's head. Then when he saw it wasn't blood, he thought it was a hoax, so he brought the evidence to me – expert on the alphabet painter's work – to weigh up while he went back on patrol.

The old man comes out of my bathroom looking

a little calmer. I help him back into the chair. Most of the paint has come off with water. It's still quite fresh. A ghost of a Q is just visible on his forehead, but that will fade in time.

'I promised you a cup of tea, George. You've had a stressful morning.'

From the kitchen, I can hear him muttering to himself, too fast to make out any words. When I come out with his drink, he has another request.

'Can I stop here for a while?'

I can understand why he doesn't want to go back on the streets, at least until Sligo is caught. But I value my privacy. I tell him I'm sorry. He says TJ has offered him a bed in Calladine's flat. That changes everything. I can't let them drag him in. I feel I have to save him from God's Anointed.

'Stay for a while then, George.'

Later, as he takes a long bath, I print him up in the darkroom. These are wonderful. Half lit by the window, his face is lined beyond even his years. His eyes are still wide and moist with terror, and a perfect Q is branded on the centre of his brow. No newspaper could fail to run this on the front page.

As I peg up the prints, I am filled with pity for him, then anger. Tired, arthritic, homeless, he had knocked himself out with drink and collapsed in the church porch for the night. He'd woken up sore as always and headed for the Market Place to beg between the cashpoints. When people began to stare, point, whisper; he'd turned and looked at his reflection in a shop window.

It was the real thing – colour, shape, artistry, all spot

on. But a new departure nonetheless. Brick, tarmac, wood, stone, iron – the fabric of the town was one thing. Skin was another. Adam Sligo crossed a line this morning. Even my sympathy is being tested. I leave the darkroom and pick up the phone to ring Alex. I can hear a faint, hollow whistling from my bathroom, as the old man tries to kid himself that everything is fine.

From the very beginning, there were Untaken Photographs. When I'd shown my mother the first fruits of my camera, I went back upstairs. I had a large scrapbook with coloured pages, where I kept old circus tickets, cuttings of cars from magazines, even a lock of my own hair. I stripped the book clean, and began to make an album of it.

I made one page for my Austin Cambridge – pristine in some prints, charred in others – and half a page for the dog. The other half I filled with shots of the bedroom at my grandmother's house. There were three pictures left. I laid them out on the bed.

In the first, most of the pond was visible and she was just a shape in the middle, like a rock among the lilies, or the base of a fountain. In the foreground on the flagstones were her shoes, neatly paired as if at the foot of a bed. I think it was chance. I don't remember placing them. For the second shot, I'd moved a little closer, and you could see it was a woman now, an elderly woman half-floating, half-submerged and tangled with weed. Her stockinged right foot was poking through some leaves like a fish coming up for air.

The third was best and worst. Somehow, I'd gathered up the courage or the hatred to go right to the edge, to grab a thick fistful of willow strands and lean out, so with one hand on the camera I got her face. It wasn't quite a close up, not the kind that fills the frame, but it was detailed. For a beginner, it was well taken. Her face, though whitening, still had a flush from the minutes of screaming my name. Her lips were slightly parted, as if to take a sip of water. Her eyes were open, but without the pinched, strained look she'd gained from years of squinting out at an untrustworthy world.

I decided there and then that I must keep them, but no one else could ever see them. I stacked the three together and hid them, curled inside the third doll of a Russian nesting set. They were grandmother dolls – an old birthday gift from her travels – so it seemed appropriate.

I was never a good sleeper. Sometimes at night I'd get the shots out and look at them. The close-up gave me nightmares, but that didn't stop me wanting to see it. When I went to Art school, I didn't take the Russian doll, so I kept them in my wallet. I had to fold them, which grieved me. As my mother got older, I couldn't risk her discovering them. I knew it would finish her.

As a student, and for the first years out on the road with my camera, I kept them with me, like some men keep pictures of their wives or kids. But I never forgot they were there, never took them for granted. If anything, their power grew with the years.

I used to worry that keeping them pocketed against my heart all day would harden it like her heart. I worried that – an unlucky charm – they would ensure that I could never trust, never love.

When I moved into this flat – alone – I stopped carrying them round. Under the darkroom floorboards would be safe enough.

On the afternoon I learned about Michelle's baby, I didn't go straight home. I left TJ with Paddy in the park and went for a walk in the edgelands. I must have walked for miles, in shock at first, then trying to figure out why this new information felt so familiar.

It was a long, late-summer afternoon, and the grasshoppers and crickets were almost deafening. I spent a good while by a small nameless lake – as clear and cool as any mountain stream – and watched the herons and gulls fishing from capsized milk crates and supermarket trolleys. I wondered what its name would be, if it had a name. It was no one's discovery, no secret, but no one ever looked at it, respected it. Behind the lake, scruffy horses grazed in and out of scrub woodlands, picking their way between hawthorns and blackberry bushes.

In those hours, I declared my love for the edgelands again. This is the last real wilderness. The rest of Britain is carved up into urban, suburban, agricultural and national park – all mapped and managed. Here, among the warehouses and rubbish tips, is a whole new nation built on a fertile bed of old soils, glass, junk, builders' rubble. Most of it is unkempt, unnamed, unwatched, unoccupied. By the end of the afternoon, I felt restored by the edgelands, by my wilderness.

When I got back, I crept past the door-with-no-locks, but there was no light, no sound. In my own flat, old man George was asleep in the spare room.

I locked myself in the darkroom and took the treasure box out from under the floorboards. Now Jake and Michelle's shots had gone, there were only three Untaken Photographs left – the first three. I didn't even glance at them, but threw two into a dry sink. Then I took a match and lit a corner of the third. It was a stupid thing to do, given the chemicals in that room. The Untaken Photographs went up with a flame that shocked me, sent me thudding back against the door. I picked up a cloth and used it as a glove to reach the cold tap, but the cloth caught fire too, burning my hand as I tried to shake it off into the sink.

By the time I flooded the sink, the smoke alarm was screeching. I heard footsteps rushing down the corridor. I just had time to poke the black, sopping twists down the plughole, and that was the end of my grandmother.

I've gone back to the map – a larger-scale map this time – in my hunt for a hidden pattern to the alphabet. I draw in the letters with a fine nib, as accurately as I can. One thing's for sure straight away: it's not a question mark. So much for TJ's theory. The letters are much too bunched, too finely clustered in the edgelands for that. I'm staring and staring.

It reminds me of afternoons spent cloud-watching as a child, lying on my back watching grey-white masses form into huge birds, sharks, boats and faces.

Once you've teased a shape out of the shapeless, it seems obvious. It could never have been anything else. And that's what I feel now, as the spidery clump of letters clarifies into a half-drawn swastika. If the painter continues his journey through the edgelands, if he takes in the gravel works, allotments, water-treatment plant, then he'll have the town marked with a swastika.

Is it just me? Are my eyes conjuring something out of nothing? It's not such a wild idea, that a loner obsessed with guns and camouflage gear, a man like Adam Sligo, might have a penchant for swastikas.

I fold the map away, and when I take it out again a day later, the letters don't look like a swastika at all. More like a ship's anchor, and a broken one at that.

Distortion Series – Image Six: It's my lookout. If I don't leave the radios on, I won't pick up the stories. They say Weegee kept the police channel on all night by his bed. He would sleep through fifteen unpromising call-outs, then be up and out in seconds for the one that showed real promise. I guess he trained his unconscious mind to pick up on certain key words.

Since my unconscious mind has chosen to stop me working on the motorways, I don't torture myself with police short wave any more. There's no point in listening to the call-outs when I know I'm not going to go.

Anyway, that night I saw the blue lights cross the edgelands, and followed them in. Following them – rather than beating them to it – has its price. I did get there, but not in good time. They were stretchering him into the back of the ambulance, and there were a few kids with skateboards hanging round to see what they could see.

What I saw was a man with his eyes closed, not dead yet, but not with us either. The ambulance men told me he'd fallen off the roof of the power station. The skateboard kids told me he was pushed, and they told me he was Adam Sligo. He was dressed in camouflage shirt and cap, and I could see his big black boots sticking out at the end of the stretcher. The kids were wrong. I'd spent a long time staring at Sligo on the video, and this guy wasn't him. There was no likeness facially, not even close. And besides, this one was shorter and fatter than the real thing.

Nonetheless, if he was pushed, he had to shoulder some of the blame himself. You don't wear that kind of outfit in the edgelands these days. Not with the town crying out for a lynching. Short of carrying a paintbrush and a can of scarlet paint, it's hard to imagine how he could have made things worse for himself.

When the ambulance had gone, the skateboard kids started spinning stories, how the poor guy was forced up on the roof at gunpoint by a gang of men in white. But their stories didn't match.

XVIII

Petra Ware called the police. Apparently, she'd gone to take the old man his shopping, and found him in front of a deafening TV as ever. She said hello, but he said nothing. Perhaps he couldn't hear her. The room was dark with the windows boarded up, but she didn't put a light on. She didn't want to shock him. She unpacked his food in the kitchen, then went back to say goodbye. Again, he said nothing. He just sat there, bathed in the changing lights of the TV screen. Unable to get an answer, she walked around and stood next to the TV, hoping he would notice her. But he didn't notice anything.

His throat had been opened, wide, as if to let all the colour out. His face was a white marble death mask and everything was dark red below the line drawn under his chin. I can picture it, but I didn't see it. It doesn't exist on film. Somewhere inside I was sorry. Sorry I'd missed it, left the radios off and missed my chance. If I'd shot it, maybe it would make more sense. The way she told it in the paper, he was sitting in the same chair as always, his arms on its arms, head back on the antimacassar, eyes open as if he didn't want to risk missing a moment of the TV show – even in death.

*

I only went back once, in my first term at Art college. For almost a decade I'd wondered what had happened to the house. My mother never told me, and I never asked. So I borrowed a car, said I was going on a shoot, and went back to see where my grandmother lived and died, where I lived and my old car died. I kept thinking that the house would still be there, and the pond, but the charred Austin Cambridge must have been broken up years ago.

I didn't go alone. I took a Chinese fellow student with me. Not many of us had chosen the lens over the brush. She was one, and she was good too. She was trying to capture aspects of Englishness. I told her that my grandfather had bought an old vicarage when he came back from Hong Kong. I told her it was deep in English countryside, surrounded by fields, streams, woods. I didn't want to face it on my own.

In the past ten years, the city had crept out. That was the first shock. What used to be a tiny hamlet in an ocean of wheat fields was now a large village surrounded by the city's edgelands. The house itself was hemmed in by a tall metal fence. The sign outside said 'School of Meditation Science', next to a silhouette picture of a figure in the lotus position. The Chinese girl asked me if my grandmother was some kind of guru. I fought the temptation to laugh. I didn't want to talk about her, just her house, her garden, and the woods out at the back.

We walked down a side alley between the old house and the new car showroom next door. At the back, the unkempt garden had been remade from scratch. The pond was filled in, and the site was mapped with gravel, white rocks and wooden pergolas covered with climbing plants. In the middle of the garden, a young man in what looked like a red dressing gown was sitting with his eyes closed on a backless wooden bench. I took a shot of him through the fence.

I remember the Chinese girl giving me a disapproving look, as if I was disturbing something sacred, private. But I wasn't. He was. His spine was too straight for sleep, so he must have thought he was meditating. It looked absurd to me, a man seeking tranquillity on the very spot where she'd drowned. Was there no echo of her screams?

I glanced up at my bedroom window, and saw the flailing limbs of a man or woman beating the hell out of a punchbag suspended from the ceiling. That's my kind of meditation. I took a shot of that too, on a long lens.

When we got to the woods, I found I couldn't speak. The Chinese girl kept asking if this was the car I had mentioned. I lavished film on it, all angles. She pointed at some spray-can writing on the roof – DAVEY KING OF THE WOODS. Underneath it, another hand had scratched out a response – WANKER. She wanted to know if I knew Davey. She looked sad, as she walked around the charred heap. But none of it mattered to me – not the graffiti, not the beer cans and fag ends in the back seat, not the missing steering-wheel and gear lever. All that mattered was that it was still here – my Austin, my Auburn, my home.

*

Up until now, I actually admired the alphabet as a work of art. I was impressed by the quality of the painting, despite some tricky locations, and I was caught up in the drama of the hunt for the next letter.

If the rumour from Sligo's house was true though, it changed everything. There was no way I could check it out for sure. Petra was an unreliable witness, and besides, she told the papers that she didn't switch the light on. She said that when she saw Sligo's father, she ran out of the house and phoned the police from a call box. Nonetheless, within days, the rumour was out that some letters were found at the scene. To be precise, they said that an S and a T had been painted on the backs of old man Sligo's hands, and a huge R on the wall above the fireplace.

There was no way I could know. My radios were off, so I didn't get there first. If I don't get there first, I don't get there at all. By the time I heard, the bungalow was a crime scene, all taped off with sentries on the door.

Alex was annoyed with me for failing to get the letters. He ran the story anyway – across the front. There was speculation about candles too, a ring of candles round his armchair when the police came in. But Petra didn't mention them in her account. Even with my radios on, it would have been a tough one. No shutterbug wants to be caught in a private house with a man who's had his throat cut.

After Jake and Michelle were murdered, something fell on the town like a fog, but after old man Sligo died, it got much thicker. Things were different. I saw less of TJ, who seemed to be body-guarding Calladine whenever he went out.

One night, I heard them coming back late. His door was open, and Calladine didn't bother to keep his voice down. TJ must have asked him a question, about where the evil had come from, but he got a rant instead of an answer. I could hear every word.

He said it was there in the town all the time. It's hereditary. We carry it like a virus, lying dormant for years, decades, producing minor symptoms we choose to ignore. He said if it hadn't been there, Adam Sligo couldn't have done what he did to Jake and Michelle. But evil can't flourish on its own. It needs someone to open a door, and that's what Adam did. When he stood in front of that old BMW and took aim at the windscreen, he was asking the forces of darkness to overrun this place. Within weeks, he was killing his own father.

Has old man George recovered from becoming a part of the alphabet? It's hard to tell. He's not living on the streets anymore, since he's in my spare room. He's not begging for food anymore, since I'm feeding him. No one's painting letters on his forehead, and the pink shadow of the Q washed off within days. But he doesn't say anything. He's polite. He'll nod and mumble please and thank you. That's it.

Over the weeks, I've got used to him, and no longer feel the pressure to get him back on the streets. When he heard about old man Sligo, he went into his room for a couple of days, and wouldn't come out to eat. I could understand that. George was the first human target of the alphabet painter. The second was Sligo's dad, with a letter on each hand, and he had his throat cut.

One effect of having a lodger who never leaves my flat is that I leave it more. I lock myself away in the darkroom, but I still hear him padding about the place. If I want solitude, I get in the car. I do a lot of cruising for the alphabet, but I don't know what to expect now. If the rumour is true that three letters appeared at old man Sligo's murder scene, then I'm looking for a U. If not, then there's been a long gap.

Before the Sligo bungalow, all recent letters appeared in the edgelands. Since it's a place I like anyway, I take to driving to the Bluebird car park, and walking round the edgelands for hours with the camera buttoned inside my coat. I don't see a scarlet U. All I see is a town on the edge. This new murder, and the letters, are getting to all of us. I'm one of the few pedestrians I see. There are more cars on the streets. People feel safer in their metal boxes. I see very few kids out on their own now, especially after dark. I can't prove it, but I think there are guns around too. At night I hear shots from behind the old warehouses, out of view of the road. Target practice in the cause of self-defence.

The police, at their latest press conference, called for vigilance, and for information. One journalist asked them if they'd had the red paint from old man Sligo's hands analysed. They wouldn't confirm that any painted letters were found at the scene.

Mister Motor's noticed the temperature rising. Even by his standards, he's putting up with a lot of rage from customers. Everyone's fuse is trimmed to nothing. The more the papers call it TOWN OF TERROR, the more people rise to meet the expectation.

My walks are like puzzles. How many routes can

you devise around the edgelands, without coming into contact with the place where Jake and Michelle died, the place where this all began? I don't want to go there, it makes me angry, and it depresses me. I avoid it for days, but the puzzle is self-defeating. The more I circle around it, the more that sad heap of flowers seems the centre of the whole place.

One morning, as I park up at the Bluebird Centre, I meet Arthur coming out. He looks self-conscious, carrying four or five bags of shopping. He nods down at them.

'A few gifts for my daughter.'

I'm wondering what kind of gifts would please Ally these days.

'That's nice,' I say.

'No camera, Perry?' I nod, and point to the bulge under my coat.

'Good,' he says. 'What are you shooting?'

'Nothing really. Just carrying it. Lost the stomach for my old work.'

Arthur tuts, and shakes his head. As he tells me that all the great photographers shot first and asked questions later, the spirit of the other Arthur – lookalike and namesake – slips into him. Here I am in a shopping-centre car park, being told off by Weegee for giving up ambulance-chasing.

'This town's on a knife-edge. A true shutterbug would capture that.'

I glance at my watch, say my goodbyes and leave. He's right, of course. A great photographer draws his own lines. Maybe conscience is like sin; give it a foothold and it floods you. Maybe all that prayer across the hallway is weakening the defences I've built up all these years. Maybe I should pray to get my motorway stomach back. Anyhow, until I do, I'm stuck with the back roads, stuck with the edgelands.

I walk around the block a few more times, then make for the Collegiate Tower. I turn the corner, and head towards the murder scene.

Distortion Series – Image Seven: It didn't come through the radios. It came by chance, as I was drifting through the edgelands at night. I saw some lights from the back of the Soccerdome. That place was well lit anyway, but this was different. The brightest lights seemed to be coming from behind the building. I looped round the car park, to see what was going on. There were trucks with searchlights trained on the nameless lake, and police frogmen on the edge. I could see a couple of divers dipping up and down like they were feeding.

I knew that lake well, and I knew how clear it was, so whatever they were looking for, I guessed they would probably find it. I got the car as close as I could, then wound my window down and took a wide shot. I knew I wouldn't get much more than that, and sure enough they saw me. One guy in uniform beckoned to another, and they ran across towards me. One of them was shouting, and holding out his hand to stop me shooting. I wanted to know what – or who – they were looking for, but I knew they weren't going to tell me, so I turned tail and went home, but not before I'd got a nice shot of the two cops coming for me.

XIX

At first, I see no sign of life at the murder scene. I haven't seen this square so empty since the night I first came down here and found Jake and Michelle in a ticking-over BMW. There's a breeze blowing the slips of prayers on the fence. I take a few paces back to think about a shot.

Then I catch sight of him. When Arthur said he'd bought gifts for his daughter, I'd assumed it was the other daughter. But here he is, kneeling in the rain, laying out what looks like a nightdress, then a white bear, then a necklace. He goes on until the bags are empty. He has his back to me, so I don't know if he's crying. He doesn't seem at all like Weegee now. Before I leave, I unbutton my coat and take a picture.

If the town's cracking up, then his family is leading the way. Here he is, an expat on both sides of the ocean, with one dead daughter, and another who wears a lot of white these days. She talks about the end of the world too, given half a chance. I don't give her the chance, of course. I practically sprint down that hallway outside my flat these days. Calladine's got Ally, no mistake. She's one of God's Anointed, and there's nothing I can do, except – as her father tells me – document it all.

*

'What do you know about that American?'

It's late, and his breath smells of whisky, though he looks cold sober. When Calladine knocked at the door, I was about to go to bed. I wasn't expecting anyone, but especially not him. He never comes to my door now. He never speaks to me, and that's just the way I want it.

'Which American?'

'You know who I mean.'

'What d'you want to know?'

'Where's he from? What's his name? What's he doing here?' He bangs on the doorframe, impatiently. I stand my ground. He's not coming in.

'Name's Arthur. From somewhere in Florida. Why's it your business?'

'Florida?'

'Ask Ally. He's her father.'

'Ally has other things to worry about.'

He shakes his head as he speaks, as if delivering a warning.

'I don't think he's on our side.'

'Why are you telling me? I'm not on your side either.'

He looks at me with pure hatred. That's him. That's the essence of Calladine. If I had a lens focused on his face, and captured this moment, it would make a picture that could bring 'God's Anointed' to their knees. But I don't have my camera. It's one of Weegee's truths that if you have your camera poised, and wait, you will see people reveal themselves. He called it 'the breathless moment', that split second when the mask drops, and you see into a person's heart. If you miss it, it may never come your way again.

As he turns to go back to his flat, he staggers and almost falls, supporting himself on the wall. He may sound sober, but his legs give him away. Without looking back at me, he pitches another question.

'What d'you say he's here for?'

'I didn't.'

My grandmother's wasn't the first dead body I set eyes on. Once, from the back of my parents' car, I saw a man standing still in the middle of a yellow field. He lifted one arm up to his head, then he hit the ground. I stared out of the back window for as long as I could, but he didn't get up. Before he hit the ground, he jolted as if he'd been punched. I told my mum and dad. They said it must have been a scarecrow. I said scarecrows don't move. They said it must have been a farmer with his gun shooting crows. They were just saying that. It might have been a farmer with his gun, but he wasn't shooting crows.

I don't remember where the field was, or where we'd been. I do remember all the way home I was thinking how simple it looked. Man stands up, man falls down. I remember wondering if it could be as simple the other way around. If life after death is as simple as death after life, then anyone can do it, anyone can have it. It's a matter of knowledge. You don't have to know how it happens, just that it does. I keep trying, and it's getting easier. Sometimes I don't know if I know it, or just think I know it.

*

No letters. Weeks now, and no flashes of scarlet across brick, stone, skin. No one is sure if the rumours were true about the R, S and T and old man Sligo.

The more I think about it, the less I can see why Adam Sligo would stop the sequence. Maybe he's just saving them up? If he is a serial killer, maybe he's planning his next attack. I wonder if the police found candles round his old man's body.

I saw the smart-looking woman from God's Anointed on my way back from photographing Arthur at the murder scene. She wasn't hard to spot, in her long white dress. She looked like a lost bride. I wondered what her hospital job was – surgeon? Nurse? Anaesthetist? Why would someone like that fall for Calladine? I imagined her telling her colleagues at work that from now on – because of her religious beliefs – she'd need white gloves, smock, overalls. In her line of work, that's like turning yourself into a blank canvas.

I let the car idle, and watched her in the rear-view mirror. She was carrying a small bunch of flowers behind her back: a ghost with a fistful of blood-coloured blooms. She looked cold, in her summer dress, as she reached the place where Jake and Michelle died, and placed her flowers alongside the wilting bouquets. She took a step back, and seemed to rub her eyes. I slipped the handbrake, and headed off as quietly as I could.

XX

I knew there was something going on, so I followed them. They don't normally gather en masse in the flat across the hallway first thing on a Saturday morning. Now I've parked a few rows away from them, and I'm zipping the camera under my jacket. All around me, there are men and women in white getting out of cars, ten or fifteen cars taking over a corner of the vast car park.

In the early morning light, the Bluebird Centre looks like a palace. The sun brings out the rich honey colour of its stone walls. All around the edge of the roof are mock-classical statues, too high up to see in detail. One of them, above the main doorway, is leaning back, stretching a bow as if to shoot the sun out of the sky. Rising from the centre of the building is a glass dome with tables being set for lunch. A fast lift connects the restaurant with the shopping floors below.

Above the dome is a blue glass bird in flight, the emblem of the Centre. It must be as big as a man, but from here in the car park it looks dazzling, fast and light, like a swallow frozen as it reaches the apex of the dome. Around the dome, real birds – gulls miles from the sea – are circling, rising and falling in an intricate repeating pattern. I've been in the Bluebird Centre countless times, but I've never really looked at it.

Che calls out for the others to hurry. He's keeping his head down and drawing deeply on a cigarette. Calladine and Maurice hand out glass bowls from a car boot. I can't see clearly what's in the bowls, but a couple of them sniff it, and turn up their noses. Calladine leads the way across the car park, towards the glittering glass front doors. I take a couple of shots through my windscreen, then get out and follow at a distance.

The Bluebird is quiet for a Saturday. Fear still keeps some people off the streets and away from the shops. Not all the shoppers are staring as God's Anointed process down the endless marble aisles. I guess some think they're promoting a product. Every now and then they hit a piazza, where four aisles meet. There are jungles, woodlands and fountains with brass birds shooting fine jets at each other in timed sequences.

But the piazza where they stop is different. Instead of a fountain in the centre, there's a racing-green E-Type Jaguar. It's behind a rope, like a museum exhibit. I've seen it before, and reached across to run a finger down its wing. It is a dream car.

Calladine gathers them all together round the car. He closes his eyes and starts muttering. It's like the muttering he used against Alex in my flat, only this time he's thrown his head back, and it's loud. They've all got their eyes shut, so I move a bit closer, get the camera out, and fire off some shots.

After a few minutes, he stops. A crowd has begun to gather, and a security guard on the floor above looks down and talks into his radio. Calladine dips a thumb into his bowl, turns to Maurice and rubs black lines across his forehead, cheeks and chin, like war paint. I think it must be ash, judging by its colour. I hear him say something about Sodom and Gomorrah, and then 'Repent'. Maurice turns and does the same to Che. They all start daubing each other with ash.

Calladine and Maurice move out among the shoppers. People are giving them a wide berth. Calladine shouts at one man, reaches out and marks his forehead, but the man knocks Calladine's arm away and shouts back something about Hare Krishna. Che comes over to put the mark on me, then recognises me and backs off. I raise the camera, but he covers his face with his hands.

Shoppers are staring at them wide-eyed, backing off as they are approached. Maurice has his bowl knocked out of his hand, and drops to his knees to try to scoop the ash back in. Calladine is getting louder, telling people time is running out.

He's right. It lasts about five minutes before the security guard on the upper floor gets the assistance he'd called for, and they're all moved on. Che disappears as soon as the guards arrive, no doubt terrified of meeting old colleagues. But Calladine is ranting all the way back to the entrance. God's Anointed slope off in different directions, wiping the ash off their faces with sleeves or handkerchiefs. TJ sticks with Calladine and I see he's got a hand in his jacket pocket.

I get a few shots of them retreating, then – pure self-indulgence – I take a few shots of the car. There's a notice round the back that I haven't see before. It says this motor is a celebration of the entrepreneurial spirit behind the Bluebird Centre. This was Britain's first and biggest mega-mall, and it was one man's dream. He died a month before it opened, but here was his beloved E-Type, as a tribute.

I can hear my grandmother's voice inside my head, lecturing again.

'See,' she says.

'See what?'

I always play dumb, though I know her point before she makes it.

'You can't take it with you.'

I've taken to walking Paddy in the dark. It suits him better, and it suits me too. The old tramp in my spare room has started singing and chanting deep into the night. The wall between our rooms is nothing but a sheet of hardboard, so I pick up everything. At first I found it maddening. I knocked on the wall the first couple of nights, and he'd stop for half an hour, then start again just as I fell asleep.

When he got up, around lunchtime, I'd ask him politely to keep the noise down, but the next night it was just as bad. In the end, he told me he was afraid to sleep, in case that devil with the blood-red paint came back to finish him. He sings hymns and murmurs prayers all night to give himself some protection.

The dog comes for me at one or two o'clock and I'm awake, watching TV or messing about in the darkroom. I've given up trying to sleep until the old man pipes down, around three o'clock or so, when sleep overwhelms his fears. Since most of the letters were found in the morning, I've always assumed that the painter works at night. If I'm out there, I might catch him, so I take a flash with me. Now that would be a picture. Even Weegee would tip his fedora to a man who shot and printed up the painting of the letter U.

The night after the Bluebird Centre mission, Paddy doesn't come to me at one, or at two. I have to go and get him. Calladine's flat is empty, and immaculate. There are no bottles anywhere in sight, no ashtrays, just a faint smell of cigarette smoke. The card table is folded against the wall, chairs with it. The sash window is open a crack and the net curtains are breathing in and out. The dog is padding up and down the room, doubling back on himself at each turn like a zoo tiger. When he sees me, he comes up and licks the back of my hand. He's never done that before. We walk out into the night together.

Tonight more than ever I long to find Adam Sligo, to catch him trying to shield his face against my flash, a brush in one hand and a half-finished U on a wall in front of him. Blinded by the flash he'd draw his gun, but I'd melt into the shadows. In fact, we see no one out on foot. Sligo wouldn't shoot me anyway. I'm the one he chose to document his work.

A couple of cars pass us. One taxi slows down and gestures to his back seat, assuming I don't want to be walking these mean streets alone at night. I point down at Paddy, but realise he isn't at my side anymore. He's run ahead into the park.

I find him whimpering, flat to the floor, about ten feet from the maned wolf's cage. I shine a torch in. As ever, there is no trace, just tall grass, weeds, a stripped bone, and the wooden kennel in the corner. I press the torch against the mesh fence and line it up to shine into the arched mouth of the kennel. Maybe there is something in there, a bright golden eye to catch the light. Nothing. Darkness.

By the time we get back to the flats, I'm feeling depressed about the alphabet. Terrifying it may be, but it is at least consistent. If the sequence stops before the end, it will make no sense. At the top of the stairs Paddy darts into the flat, and starts barking with excitement. I hear Calladine's voice gently shushing him.

I try to remember her mouth. I keep thinking about the moments before I took the first shot. Did her lips move? Did she let out one last word above the low tick of the engine? I've been replaying it over and over in my mind. Is it possible that Michelle did say 'Shanty'?

After days of mulling it over, I begin to believe that she could have said something. Not 'Shanty', because I distinctly recall making that up. But I wonder if I conjured it from nowhere, or found it in the echo of the real last words of Michelle. It could have been 'Save me'. That would make sense. If I close my eyes, I can see her with her head on Jake's shoulder. She's looking at me, and yes, she could be saying something with her last breath.

If it was 'Save me', then I did it in the only way I could. She was way beyond medical help. Her life could not be saved. And I couldn't save her soul, because I didn't know what that meant. So I took her into my camera, and saved her there. I preserved her in her last moments.

I need my prints back. Even though I destroyed the close-ups of Michelle, there are wide shots of them both, and close-ups of Jake. Thanks to Michelle's father, all those shots are out of my hands. I have to get them back. If Michelle asks me to save her, then that's what I should do. I should have kept those shots safe under the darkroom floorboards. My Untaken Photographs – they should have stayed that way.

It's past three in the morning, so Calladine is right to try to shush the dog. Not that it will disturb the neighbours, since I'm awake anyway, and my lodger is too terrified to sleep. As I walk past the door, I see Paddy jumping at his master, who is standing by the fireplace with his coat on.

'I wondered where you'd gone.'

At first I think he's talking to me, but he's looking at the dog. I don't think he's seen me. I creep along the corridor and slip the key into my own front door. George is singing quietly in the spare room: *Be Thou still my strength and shield*. I'm tired and should go to bed, but instead I stand still for a moment – listening – then creep back out of my room and into the dark hallway. I set myself up in the shadows facing his open door.

Calladine unscrews the cap on a whisky bottle, then screws it back on and puts the bottle down. He unfolds the chairs that go with the card table, and sets them facing each other in the middle of the room. The dog lies down in front of the fireplace, drawn by some memory of heat, though I've never seen it lit.

Calladine sits down and stares into the cold grate. I've got spare film in my pockets, a flash, and there are good strong lights in the room. As quietly as I can, I frame up a portrait. I'm only interested in close-ups. If you're going to make a portrait, you should go for the eyes and mouth. Eyebrows at the top of the frame, chin at the bottom. Then you stand a chance of catching something of the essence. Even in a photograph – especially in a photograph – there's life in the eyes of the living. It's not just because they're looking straight at you. It works even when they're not.

He rubs his eyes with the back of his hand. He's taken his coat off to reveal a white linen suit. It must have been expensive, but it looks very crumpled now, and there are darker patches on it. His hands are shaking, and they break into the frame as they wipe his eyes. Before long he's crying, really sobbing, and I close in on the framing.

As I line up, I know I'm only going to get one shot. A face when crying, a face that believes it's unobserved, goes through multiple variations in expression. I'm spoilt for choice. And I'm wondering who, or what, the tears are for. Are they tears of humiliation, since he was ignored and thrown out of the Bluebird? Are they tears of loneliness, of self-pity, of fear?

How subtle, how infinitely gentle the push of a button can be, as I edge towards the single, perfect portrait. Suddenly – despite my utter silence – something makes him look up. For a split second he stares right at me. His gaze bolts straight through the lens, out the back of the camera and into me. He's challenging me to cry too. Whatever it is, he wants me to feel it. But I can't and I won't.

I press the button and the flash loops the narrow hallway, then I turn and run back to my flat, locking the door behind me. He hammers and shouts, but I don't respond.

I know it's a great picture, and I'm glad I've got it, but that doesn't mean I'm not scared. I never joined him, but now, for the first time I've crossed him. All I hope is that I don't get a punishment visit from the men in white. I've seen what they do to people who break their rules.

XXI

I've now heard that story from so many angles, but the only one I can tell is my own. It was a bright morning. Everyone says that. In fact, it was dazzling. I had my sunglasses on as I went past the Bluebird on my way to Mister Motor. I was keen to get there. I hadn't seen Mister M for weeks, and he's good company, but most of all I wanted to see the car. He'd given me a call the night before, and said he had the old blue BMW. Would I be interested in taking a look?

Would I? I never dreamt I'd see it again. To set eyes on it might spark some memory of that other dazzling day, the day that began this extraordinary summer. Maybe a glimpse of that metallic blue, or the smell of the old leather seats, could bring Michelle's last words back to me. I'd been replaying in my head the two or three minutes I spent with Jake and Michelle before the police came. It was all still very clear, except the moment I moved in for the close-ups, when I framed up on Michelle's face. Were her lips moving? I was less and less sure.

I pulled into Mister M's and had my pick of the parking bays. No happy customers yet. He tends to get busier as the day goes on. The man himself was pleased to see me, and even the boy Anthony managed a nod. He asked Anthony to mind the desk and he took me out the back. He looked pleased with himself.

'As soon as it came in, I knew you'd wanna to see it.'

'Why have you got it?'

'Cops have done with it.'

We walked between stacks of cars as tall as houses. In the corner of the yard, standing on its own, was an old dark blue BMW. It looked a bit beaten up, but not crash-damaged. The windscreen was shattered. There wasn't much wrong with it. Crushing seemed a waste.

He opened the passenger door and stood back like a chauffeur. At first, I shook my head, but he said it was okay. By the end of the day, this car would be a cube. I sat down in Michelle's seat, and waited for the memory to kick in.

The more I remembered, the more sure I was that this was a different car. The dashboard was cleaner, better kept. No scratches and tears like Jake's. The upholstery was a different shade, and there wasn't a trace of blood.

'They've cleaned it up, of course.' He could see I wasn't convinced.

'Why would they clean it up to crush it?'

'Part of the investigation, picking up the evidence.'

I got out of the car and walked around it. Then I stood and faced Mister Motor.

'What are you up to?'

'How d'you mean?'

'This isn't Jake's car.'

I remembered him opening his mouth, looking

slightly indignant, but no sound came out. The next ten minutes or so are stored in my memory as freeze frames. I can step through them in order.

One: Mister M is standing with his mouth open, and there's a massive explosion from over the fence behind his yard. I can feel it under my shoes, in my guts. I feel winded. I feel like I've been punched in the heart.

Two: We're both staring at a spreading stain of smoke across the sky above the Bluebird Centre dome. Anthony has stepped outside, he's looking across at us, shouting, 'What the fuck?'

Three: Mister M is messing with a padlock on the tall metal gate that opens from his yard onto the Bluebird Centre car park. He can't get the key in the slot. Anthony is jabbering, but I'm not listening. I'm watching the smoke rise. In the car park, people are standing with bags of shopping, gazing back at where they've just been.

Four: We're not running, more like jogging. We don't know what we're heading into. We're about fifty yards from the front entrance, and I can see inside. It's all smoke. A woman rushes out. Her head is cut, her face and coat are stained with blood and black marks. She's screaming, running towards us. For a second, probably less than a second, I remember my camera in the car and wish I had it with me. In that fraction of a second I think of Nick Ut.

Five: A young security guard pushes us back from the doors with aggression born of terror. He looks pretty unscathed himself, so I guess he was near this door when it happened. Through the glass, I can see more people, or shadows of people, moving through the smoke towards the exit. There's screaming inside, and fire alarms.

Six: People are staggering out of the entrance, gasping for air. The young security guard has been joined by an older female colleague. They are trying to organise things, sending walking wounded to the grass bank across the car park. There's so much shouting going on that no one really hears them. They look as if they've rehearsed this. They've done drills, but nothing has prepared them.

Seven: Close to us, two teenage boys lay out a woman who could be their mother. As they carry her towards us, Mister Motor spreads his coat out on the tarmac. She looks dead to me. Her face is badly damaged. I see Anthony wince and turn to face the other way. Her sons look a bit bloody, but it's hard to tell what's theirs, and what's their mother's. One of them shouts to the other, 'What do we do?'

Eight: Blue lights everywhere. Police pushing people back, sending onlookers like us away. They're much better at marshalling than the security guards. We're through Mister M's back gate and he clicks the big padlock shut.

All afternoon, I stay in my flat and watch the news. I've got the police radios on, but there isn't much after the first hour. The old man comes out of my spare room where he hides most of the time. He sits on the sofa next to me and watches in horror. Through my window looking out across the edgelands, we can see the smoke shape in the sky, the same shape as the one on TV. When we hear a siren on the TV, we hear it through the window too. The old man is shaking. Every now and then he rubs at an itch on his forehead where the Q once was. All across the town people are putting the bomb down to Adam Sligo. Even the TV drops hints. They have nothing to lose. A killer on the run is unlikely to sue them for defamation.

By late afternoon, the flat across the hallway is filling up. I can hear them chanting and praying. I hear one or two of them asking where Calladine is, as they come in, but it seems he's gone missing again.

I'm more concerned about another absence. I can't find Paddy anywhere. Perhaps the dog went away with him. Perhaps he resents the fact that the dog has grown closer to me than to him.

What surprises me is that TJ is around. I can hear his voice. TJ sticks to Calladine wherever he goes, hands in both jacket pockets fingering his guns. If Calladine has gone away without him, then that is strange.

It's late. I'm in the darkroom because I've seen all the news I want to see for one day. The old man is singing to ward off the devil, or the alphabet painter, or both. The dog has vanished, so I'm not going to get my night-time trip to the park. All I want to do is work. Since the alphabet dried up, and I can't stomach the motorways, the only work I have to do is printing last night's portrait of Calladine.

I have to say, I'm good. Very good. Most people frame

too wide. They don't have the nerve to get in tight, and their subjects expect a bit of distance, especially if they're paying. A bit of distance hides a multitude of blemishes, but it keeps the soul hidden. A true portrait – eyebrow to bottom lip – is an intimate thing. Without a camera, I would have been that close to maybe four or five people in my life. With the box between us, it runs to hundreds. There's nothing I know about people, nothing that's worth knowing, that I didn't learn through a camera lens.

This is beautiful. He's looking into me, through the box and into me, even through these wet prints as I pull them from the tray. And there's a hint of that evil, that hatred I saw when he stood at my front door the other night. It's not the breathless moment, it's not the full glare of the soul, but it's enough.

There's still no sign of the man himself. Maybe he was caught in the Bluebird blast. Perhaps he'd gone back to try another mission there. I peg out the print and bend down to look him directly in the eyes. At that moment, I know he's gone for good. I don't know where he is, but the fact of his absence is as silent and sudden as a snowfall. I remember waking up to white drifts as a child, wondering how I'd missed the coming of something so solid and sure. Now, his vanishing seems absolute. I can't believe I didn't expect it.

Perhaps because the old man in my spare room was singing all night long. Because I hadn't had a good night's sleep for weeks. Because I couldn't find the dog to walk. Because there was enough moonlight to see the smoke still lifting from the Bluebird. Because I had a sore back and couldn't sit still. I wish I could give a single simple reason.

All I can say is that I had a hunch. I drove to the edgelands on the night after the blast, parked the car near Mister Motor's, crawled through a hedge, avoided the police on all entrances, dodged the security cameras on the doors and loading bays, and started to scan the walls of the Bluebird Centre. I shone a torch up and down every inch of brick, until I found it, perfect and unmistakeable. I framed up on the U with a flash, and took six shots of it.

XXII

Distortion Series – Image Eight: The grapevine said that someone had broken into the Territorial Army barracks at night and lifted a stack of guns and ammunition. I drove down as soon as I heard, and sure enough there were police cars parked outside, with a young cop on the door.

Of course, the rumour was that it was Sligo building up his arsenal for a final assault on the town. On the other hand, those weapons could be spread across dozens of houses. Like a lot of small market towns, this one has something of the Wild West about it. No matter how urban and civilised they think they are, when there's the slightest whiff of danger the people of this place hole up like survivalists, armed with whatever they can get their hands on.

When the chips are down, they'll defend themselves, their families, their homesteads, to the last bullet.

He'd had a few calmer nights in my spare room, and the weather had been dry and warm. I thought it was time he put a toe in the water again. We'd talked it over, and old George had agreed that he couldn't stay in my flat for ever. Having said that, he wasn't overly keen to leave, so the deal was that he'd vacate my flat for a night or two, and see how he got on.

He seemed almost persuaded by my argument that the Q on his head was a kind of inoculation. He'd been touched by the alphabet now – like I had – and it hadn't done him any harm. If he'd been marked for some damage, it would have come his way by now, whether or not he was hiding in my flat. So now he'd been immunised, George was actually safer than pretty much anyone else out there.

My heart sank when I heard him gibbering and puffing up the stairs. He'd only been out five hours and he was begging me not to make him leave the flat again. His story was that he had headed for the park and found a bench that he had always liked. It was under the shelter of a broad-leaved tree, a little way off the beaten track. He'd had a drink or two to help him sleep, and had just closed his eyes when he was threatened by ghosts.

'By what?'

'Ghosts. Three of them. They told me to get off the streets, or they'd break my arms and legs.'

'What did they look like?'

'White. They were ghosts.'

'And did they drive off in a ghostly pickup truck?'

Apparently, it started to crack as he was trying to give a rallying speech. In the absence of Calladine, Maurice – as chief sidekick – was called up to the front at one of their meetings to give them a lead. When his voice began to falter, they all thought he was nervous, but then he started coughing. The more he coughed, the more his voice weakened. Someone fetched him a glass of water, Maurice coughed hard, as if punishing his voice for failing. He drained the glass, then opened his mouth again. His voice was a croak. Then a fragmented note like a cracked reed. Finally it broke into a whisper.

I stuck my head round the door to look for the dog and saw TJ staring out of the window. Everyone else had gone. I invited him back for a drink, and that's when he told me about Maurice. For TJ, this was a sign that the powers of darkness were gaining the upper hand in the town. Calladine was missing, and the miracle of Maurice's voice was unraveling.

My old lodger was shut in his room. It was getting dark now, the start of his song time. Sure enough, he struck up as the light fell. For once it was a song I recognised. It was one of one of the songs I used to hear drifting across the hallway.

TJ was coughing, as if he'd caught it from Maurice. He lit a cigarette. 'Jesus gonna make up my dying bed,' sang the old man. TJ coughed some more.

'And yours . . .' I got a laugh out of him. He took a gun from his coat and smacked it down on the table. I took a print out of my pocket and put it on the table next to the gun. It was a shot of the U on the Bluebird wall.

'What?' He dropped the cigarette from his mouth onto his lap, grabbed it and brushed himself down. 'What is this?'

'You can see what it is.'

'But where did you get it?' He was starting to cough again, so he took a deep drag – it seemed to help.

'I took it. I took the picture.'

He picked it up, and angled it towards the light. 'How did you find it?'

I don't know if it was his love of the Auburn 851, or his grief – poured out to Mister Motor – over the death of his mum, but I couldn't find it in myself to hate Adam Sligo. Most of the town despised him, retrospectively accusing him of every crime from petty theft to rape. There was a kind of logic to it. If a man was evil enough to kill a pair of teenage lovers almost point blank, then cut his own father's throat, then blow up dozens of people in a shopping centre, nothing was out of his range.

There have been claims of sightings in town, on dark side streets at night. One taxi driver said he'd driven past the Sligo bungalow, a few nights before the old man died, and seen someone leaving the place. A man, he said, a young man in dark clothes.

To me, Adam has become part of the edgelands. He lives at the edge of all our minds, like some shy creature flitting across our peripheral vision. Many times I think I've seen him running between buildings, or sleeping under hedges.

At dawn, as the first allotment holders pick their way between the cane-rows and trellises, they beat a rhythmic chime with old bits of piping. It rings out for miles. They never used to do that, and it isn't meant to scare away the foxes. They are each convinced that Sligo sleeps the night in their makeshift fibreboard tool sheds. They do it to flush him out.

I looked long and hard for the V. My instinct was right about the placing of the U, but that wasn't hard. Whatever the alphabet painter was up to, the Bluebird on the night of the bomb was the obvious location.

There was nothing so obvious about the glass corner of Collegiate Tower. Maybe the painter thought it would look striking, and everyone would see it there, against the silver background of the glass wall. But this wasn't about aesthetics. In fact, the aesthetics this time weren't up to the usual standard. It was a slick and slippery surface, but even so, I'd come to expect a certain clarity of line, a balanced symmetry of shape in these letters. This looked a little rushed, a little ragged around the edges. Nonetheless, the colour was spot on – I had no doubt it was the real thing.

I took my shots and left just as the cleaners turned up in their van to strip the red V off the glass. Perhaps he'd been interrupted, I thought. Maybe this time, someone caught him in the act. Either that, or he was losing his touch.

XXIII

There is no need for the blue lights, but it adds to the drama of their visit. I don't want to go and strike up conversation, but I can't slip away either, because I guess they might be paying me a visit too. I want to keep busy, so I clean out my darkroom, throwing away old prints and negs, tidying my shelves and scouring the sink. As I work, I listen to the flat across the hallway being torn apart.

After half an hour, I hear them go to Che, then they come to me. There are two policemen and a young policewoman. She makes a cup of tea and sits with me while they take my flat to pieces. They sift through the bin-bag I've just filled with darkroom rubbish. My copy of Che's Sligo video is safe beneath the darkroom floorboards.

I tell them I am not a member of God's Anointed. I tell them I have nothing to do with that flat. I tell them I don't know where Calladine is, or why he's gone. I tell them the only link I have with him is that I sometimes walk his dog.

The policewoman tries to make small talk, but I'm not interested. Her colleagues aren't too careful. I think they must know what I do — used to do — for a living. My framed poster of *Napalm*, back on the wall for a few weeks, is nudged off its hook and shatters on the wooden floor.

After their fruitless search, the two men leave and the woman's talk gets serious. She puts a tape in my video machine. It's a high-angle security camera, focused on the Bluebird's main atrium. The policewoman stands by the screen and traces the path of a man with his back to us, walking quickly towards the Jag. He gets something out of his pocket – a hammer by the looks of things – and smashes the driver's window. He reaches in, and opens the door. He's wearing a backpack. People are stopping to watch, wondering what he's doing. A security guard walks in from the side, but just as he reaches the man, there's a flash, and the film ends. The sequence lasted about twenty seconds.

'Rewind it.' She wants to talk, but I need to see it again first. She presses the buttons and I watch it one more time. She waits. I say nothing.

'That's the man who did it, Perry.' She comes back to sit next to me.

'The suicide bomber?'

She nods.

'Do you know who it is, Perry?'

'Yes. Yes, I do.'

We both stare at the screen. We leave the tape running, but there is nothing on it, just shash, the snowstorm of naked TV. It's like staring into a fire, looking for pictures, shapes.

If the placing of the V was hard to predict, the W was even tougher. It would never have crossed my mind at the time, but once I'd thought about it, there was a kind of logic at work there.

All afternoon, they were up and down the stairs, carrying chairs, boxes. I guessed they were preparing for a crisis meeting. With their leader missing, his sidekick Maurice voiceless and lost, and the police sniffing around, it was hard to see any kind of future for them.

Maybe they were praying with their eyes closed. Maybe they were chanting aloud too, so they missed it when it happened. The door, was open and unlockable, so it didn't present too much of a challenge. Sometime that evening, between about seven and nine, someone took Ally's long white coat off the back of a chair near the door. They didn't take it for long, but when they put it back, it wasn't just white anymore.

It was very late. I'd been messing with my vintage Swiss camera again, trying to get some shots of fruit this time: a bunch of grapes, slightly tarnished and misted, just starting to shrivel. But I couldn't get the light right, couldn't get it stark enough. I couldn't get the clarity I felt it needed. I left the kit out, resolved to try again first thing in the morning, when the sun would be strong through my windows. I decided to leave the curtains open and sleep in the chair by the camera so I wouldn't miss the early light.

In my dream I was Weegee, out at night on the streets of a brutal city. I could hear the sounds of fights, lovers' quarrels, car smashes and hold-ups, but I couldn't see a thing. I pointed my camera into the void, and flashed. For a split second, I could see. That glimpse gave me some geography, so I crossed a road, then took another shot; moved into a building, took another; came back outside, took another. Then it struck me that it wasn't dark at all. When the flash went, the streets I saw weren't full of pimps, gangsters, nightbirds. They were full of shoppers, families with kids, office workers. It was noon-bright, but I was blind. So blind was I, that even in the full glare of daylight I needed a flashgun to see anything.

I woke up suddenly. I'd opened my eyes because I felt something. It was very early dawn. Paddy was sniffing at my hand and then sniffing at the floor around my feet. In the milk light he looked radiant, as he had when I'd first seen him in the edgelands. His coat and eyes were the brightest objects in the room. I was glad to see him back. How he got in, I didn't know. My door was shut, and locked.

'What the fuck is this?'

Arthur holds up Ally's long white coat. There's a perfect scarlet W on the back of it. He throws it down, opens my living-room window, and takes a deep draught of night air. Then he gets out a soft pack of cigarettes and lights up.

Behind us, in my spare room, I can hear the old man gibbering with terror. He thinks his worst nightmare has come true. A man breaks into our flat at the crack of dawn and starts ranting about painted letters.

'Can I just go and calm him down?'

Arthur shuts his eyes and nods. I ask him for a cigarette. He lights one, and I take it to the old man. A couple of minutes later I'm sitting down opposite Arthur, who's messing with his petrol lighter;

striking it, then flicking the lid down, striking and flicking.

'How's Ally?'

I know the answer, but I ask anyway. I've heard God's Anointed going crazy for hours across the hallway with chants and prayers and prophecies. TJ came and warned me to keep my head down – they were ready for a full-on battle with Sligo, now that he'd made Ally a target.

'Well, how the fuck d'you think she is?'

'I've had a letter on my car, and I didn't come to any harm.'

'No harm? A killer puts his mark on her coat, but there's no harm in it?'

I wondered who had given the order. I guess it must have felt like a betrayal. More than that, it must have felt like an admission, a final acceptance that Calladine wasn't coming back.

It took an hour or so for the locksmith to cut a new hole and fit an un-pickable five-lever lock. He finished the flat across the way, then I heard him go and do the same on Che's front door.

XXIV

Alex has done well out of me. He's crime reporter for the *Post* now. His jackets and trousers never used to match, but now he has a dark suit on. His hair is much shorter, and he's taking shorthand with a smart fountain pen. I don't owe him any favours. I've done more for his career than he ever did for mine. I've given him the alphabet – shot by shot – and plenty more too. He used to come to see me, but now I get a call to pay a visit to his office.

We're in a glass-walled meeting room. Outside I can see a couple of his colleagues looking at me. I should never have come. He's softening me up for something, talking about the motorways, asking if I've got some shots of yesterday's fatal. Then he gives me some news.

'You may not know yet, but this morning, the police made an arrest for the murder of Sligo's father.'

'Who?'

'Jake Ware's mother.'

'Right.'

'They found the knife in a lake near the Soccerdome.'

A girl walks up to the glass door and knocks. Alex holds up a hand and mouths the word 'five'. Then he continues.

'I have a hunch Petra Ware's the one behind the

alphabet too. If you look at the map, most of them are in places where her son had some connection.'

I'm shifting in my seat, waiting for the gear change in the conversation. When it comes, it's not the smoothest.

'Perry, you and I have worked together for a long time.'

I nod, but I don't want to say anything.

'We both understand the business. What it takes.' He pours two plastic cups of water from a jug on the table, and slides one across to me. I sip it, it's warm. It tastes of dust. He takes a drink of his, screwing up his face, trying to get me smiling. I'm not smiling.

'Perry, you know what the cops think about the Bluebird bomber?'

'No, I don't.'

'It was Calladine.'

I take another sip of the dust water and glance towards the door, wishing I was on the other side of it.

'I'm trying to help here. You give me shots of this God's Anointed group, and I'll do you a favour.'

'What kind of favour?'

'There are people out there calling this a cult. They're blaming everything that's happened to this town on your people. And now it looks as though . . .'

'They're not my people! I've got nothing to do with them!' I'm hammering the table with a fist.

'I know Perry. I'm on your side. But you live next door, and you've got connections. You can see how people might . . .'

'I've got nothing to do with them!'

'Give me some shots, Perry, and I'll vouch for that.'

An older man in shirtsleeves peers through the glass and knocks. He has a pile of newspapers tucked under his arm. Alex holds up both hands to the guy, then stands up. I can see he doesn't want to be rushed, but he's run out of time.

'Give me some shots, Perry, and I'll make it worth your while.'

'They won't come cheap.'

'We pay well. You know that.'

There is one more question I'm waiting for. I know it will come, but I can see him holding on to it, turning it in his mind, trying to make it sound as casual as possible. He saves it until we're about to leave the room, just as he's shaking my hand.

'You haven't got any shots of the man himself?'

I don't know what to make of this, so I'll set it out simply, as it happened, and I'll make no comment on the how and why.

The next location came in a dream, as a gift. It was the African dream again. I know it so well, it comes with less of a twist now, less of a rush of adrenalin when I wake up. This time, when I take my place in the line of villagers, I keep my feet dry. There's just enough space between the queue and the river for my polished brown brogues. I'm waiting for the bundle to reach me, not with fear, but with impatience. I know what it is, and I know what to do with it. Nonetheless, it is a surprise when it comes, because painted on its forehead is a red X. I lift the bundle up, and kiss the baby. The paint is still wet, and a trace of it comes off on my lips. It doesn't taste like paint, more like dust.

It seemed clear to me, when I woke up, that the X would appear in the cemetery, where Michelle's ashes were laid. Somehow, I've got so tuned in to the mind of the alphabet painter, that my subconscious is a step ahead of him, anticipating his next move before he even thinks of it.

It was all very cloak and dagger. TJ handed me a book in a padded envelope at my front door one night, saying he'd been given the book for safekeeping, but he wanted me to see it now.

'This should explain everything,' he said, as he passed me the package.

It didn't. What it did explain was the dog's name. According to the book, young Patrick broke free from slavery in Ireland and stowed away on a ship of dogs on its way to France. Dogs were the cargo, and a vicious, hungry cargo at that. But the boy Patrick had them eating out of his hand, giving him their warmth, comfort, protection. He had something of the cur in him too, a wild streak that stood him in good stead when he grew up.

So I could see why you might call a dog Paddy, but the book still begged more questions than it answered. It had Calladine's name inside the cover, and was clearly well thumbed. The word 'Saint' in the title *Saint Patrick's Confession*, had been crossed out, and various passages underlined in pencil. Most of these seemed to be about prayer. Prayer and sin. There was a lot about how often, and how fervently, Saint Patrick prayed and sinned, but it meant nothing to me.

It was not a cold night, but the wind was gusting between the upright stones. Because the murder scene had been the focus for the grief, and gifts, and visits, this cemetery – the last resting place of Jake and Michelle – was almost always empty.

I walked as quickly as I could up the slope to the memorial garden in the corner. On the triangle of grass beneath the yew trees was a planting of small wooden crosses with names on, like the names of newly planted seeds. Some of them had photographs, but the shots of Jake and Michelle bore no relation to the last shots I took of them. Pictures on graves always strike me as bizarre, the broad grins or proud stares of birthday parties, weddings, graduations now used in death to help remind us that they lived, loved, smiled, relished life. But the more I see smiles on gravestones, smiles in newspaper shots of the missing and the murdered, the more it has the reverse effect on me. Every wedding mugshot is a grave shot in waiting.

Just as I'd expected, Michelle's picture had been defaced with two scarlet diagonals across her face. I knelt down to examine the brushwork. It looked a little rushed again. He'd tried to tidy up the edges of the X, but they weren't spot on.

I took one pace back, and crossed myself, from head to heart, shoulder to shoulder. I've never done it before, but it felt right. Under my breath, I said a sort of prayer, a kind of goodbye to the baby.

His eyes widen as he sees it. He is trying to play things cool, but he can't keep his eyes in check. Alex knows a good shot when he sees it, and this is a fine one indeed. I'd say it's one of the most penetrating portraits I've ever taken. No, I'd say it's one of the best I've ever seen.

'You interested then?' I smile as he looks up from the print of Calladine.

'Oh, yes. I think we can make you an offer for this.'

I smile. 'I bet you're dreaming up the caption now, aren't you?'

'Forget captions, Perry. This is front page.'

XXV

It's a lesson I'll remember: always read appendices.

St Patrick's Confession, Appendix Two: 'What were Patrick's Alphabets?'

At key moments as he moved across pagan Ireland, the saint describes an unusual ritual.

'When the arguing with tribal chiefs was over, I would gather everyone around the sacred grove or mound. Then I exorcised and blessed salt, exorcised and blessed wine, exorcised and blessed water, exorcised and blessed ashes. Twelve candles or fires were lit around the site, and all this in a round of songs and chants.

Then I called the crowds to silence. Absolute silence. All they could hear was the wind, the flicker of the twelve flames, and the sound of their own souls turning. Slowly, I wrote them an alphabet.'

According to Appendix Two, the world of ancient Celtic scholarship is bitterly divided on the meaning of this ritual.

The *Literacy Tools* camp believes Patrick wrote alphabet tables for each new tribe he converted. If they didn't have words, they didn't have the Word. His alphabets were teaching tools, probably carved in wood.

The *ABC of Good Living* camp believes Patrick gave his new converts a guide to the basics of Christian morality, to keep them on the straight and narrow when he'd gone. The alphabet was a convenient structure for getting his message across.

The *Claiming Pagan Ground* camp is the one that gets my vote. They say the alphabets were nothing to do with teaching. They say that far from being vehicles to get pagans reading and writing, or to remind them not to covet their neighbour's wives, Patrick's alphabets were acts of great and particular power. Scratched in the soil with the end of his staff, the complete sequence of letters was a way of claiming pagan ground – and the people who lived on it – for the new faith. This was not symbolism. This was more than mere ritual. By the act of writing an alphabet across a particular piece of land a place could be transformed.

A week after Ally got the W on her coat, she and her father turn up on my doorstep again. His mood is different from the previous visit. He even shakes my hand as he comes in. Ally looks pale, uncertain as ever. The first thing I see is that she isn't wearing white.

I offer them some coffee, but Arthur says they aren't staying. They have come to say goodbye. He is taking his daughter back to the States with him, back to Florida. He wants her to start again.

'Before we leave, there's something I need to tell you.'

I swallow hard. Whatever it is, I feel I don't want

to hear it. Ally goes into the kitchen to get herself a glass of water. Arthur pulls me over by the window, and leans in face-to-face. He looks more like Weegee than ever. Is he sure his surname isn't Fellig? Did Weegee have kids? Grandkids? He whispers so close I can smell his breath.

'Evil.'

I back off, to put a little distance between him and me. Ally is standing in the kitchen doorway, sipping at her water. She says nothing.

'That man Calladine. You know what I'm saying? It was black magic. You should hear the things Ally's been telling me.'

I say nothing. Arthur looks at Ally, hoping she'll pitch in, but she turns and goes back in the kitchen. I hear her twist the tap and fill her glass over and over, washing it out.

'Only good news is, that evil bastard blew himself up before he had a chance to finish the curse.'

'The what?'

'You know what it was, you've been documenting it.'

'You don't think Sligo was painting the letters?'

'Oh come on!'

I keep my eyes down. After a minute of silence, Arthur calls Ally out of the kitchen. She follows him through the flat and I watch from my door as they walk down the corridor. He kicks at Calladine's front door as he walks past, but it has a good lock on it now.

As he turns to go downstairs, I call after him.

'Arthur, can I have my pictures back?'

'They're not yours, Perry. She was mine. They belong to me.'

I know he's not going to hand them over, but I'm worried. I don't know what it does to a father to carry round a shot of his daughter's murder scene, but my guess is that sooner or later it will finish him.

Ally pauses at the end of the corridor and looks back at me. I feel she wants me to say something, so I do.

'You're safe now.'

She keeps staring at me for what seems like minutes, but it must have been seconds. I hear her father call upstairs after her.

'Shanty,' she says, as she turns to follow him.

There's a story of a poor man who prays to win the lottery. He wants to win the jackpot, says he'll give a big chunk of it to charity, just keep a little for himself. At the end of his prayer, he hears a voice in his head telling him his prayer will be answered.

He waits for a year, and by Christmas he's getting angry. He's still homeless and hopeless. He goes into a church one afternoon, and stands in front of the altar. He shouts at God for not honouring his promises. But he gets that same voice in his head again. 'The deal's still on, but you have to buy a lottery ticket.'

So that's what I'm doing. As I tune in all my radios again, I'm buying a lottery ticket. As I drive out towards the motorway, I'm buying a ticket. As I slip down the back roads and leave the car, as I run up a farm track, as I scale the grass verge that separates the motorway from the farm, I'm buying a ticket.

I get to the top and fall to my knees. My God. Even Weegee would sink to his knees faced with this. The early morning mist looks like stage smoke, the survivors like ghosts. I've seen it all before, but not for some time. I'd forgotten the soundtrack, the noise of the living crying out in grief, pain and shock.

Speed. The house of Weegee was built on quicksand, not on solid ground. He was in and off the scene before the cops clapped eyes on it. I'm down. One, two, three shots. The motor drive is purring in my hand. This is good. I pray that my stomach will hold so I can do my job.

It even holds when I see what caused the pile-up. In the middle of what looks like Mister Motor's yard, transplanted to the motorway, there's a body on the road. Not a body flung out through a windscreen, but a piece of flatmeat, roadkill, barely recognisable as human.

I'm Weegee now, looking up at the bridge above me, muttering the words 'dry diver' under my breath. I'm snapping away. In one of the smashed cars there's an injured man screaming that he's killed someone. He or she must have dropped out of the sky in front of him, like some over-ripe fruit.

I'm saying nothing. The man is screaming, and his wife is dead in the seat next to him. It crosses my mind to put the camera down and tell him that the police are coming, an ambulance is on its way. But the first rule is say nothing. As soon as you put down the camera you are face-to-face with it, and then you've lost the privilege. At that moment, you become a voyeur.

I take one last shot, of the dry diver who started the whole thing. It's unusable, too gruesome for any newspaper. A couple of websites might take it, but I won't print it up. I take the shot as a test of my stomach, and it holds. Even as I catch a glint of gold in the mulch of flesh and fabric, some remnant of a wedding ring perhaps, it still holds.

I'm back over the grass verge in seconds, and down the other side. Still no sirens. I throw the camera into the back of my car and take the paint out. Over the verge again, and as the blue lights start to pulse on the horizon, I'm painting a large scarlet Y on the bonnet of a silver saloon.

'I did it on impulse. It seemed right. I'm sorry.'

'It was not what we agreed.'

'No, it wasn't. I'm sorry.'

'If I'd known you were going to do that, I wouldn't have . . .'

'. . . passed the mantle on to me, I know.'

I usher TJ in, because this is dangerous stuff to be discussing on my front doorstep. I knew he'd be cross with me for painting the Y. That's why I'm telling him now, so he doesn't see it in the papers for the first time. I get him a drink, and try to calm him down.

TJ is happy not to do the painting himself. Without Calladine, he'd tried to keep it going, but he knew his technique wasn't good enough. I've copied the style as accurately as possible. I have photographs of all the early letters, so I model my brushwork on them. TJ wants me to do the lettering, while he rides shotgun, artist's bodyguard.

'But I do expect to have a say on where the letters go.'

'Of course, TJ.' I hang my head. There are no excuses.

'We can't just do it on the spur of the moment.'

I tell him I think my Y is in the spirit of Patrick's alphabets. If this whole thing is about reclamation, if we're rescuing the town, then the motorway needs to be a part of it. I hope at least he'll agree with me on that. We have one more letter left. We shake hands on a promise that neither of us will complete the alphabet without the other.

The choice of a final location is going to be tough. There's no clear pattern. I'm not Calladine, don't want to be. I don't understand him. But I understand the alphabet now, and I feel the town needs it. My hunch is that we should finish in the edgelands. At least there I know the territory. With the gunman at my side, I'm confident I can complete the job.

It just shows, you should always trust your nose. I knew all along that this alphabet had something beautiful about it. The letters were following disaster, never leading it. Just because Calladine went off the rails, that doesn't mean it's not worth finishing the work. In fact, it's more vital than ever.

I saw the shrine being cleared. I photographed the whole process, as men with thick gloves and fluorescent jackets threw the heaps of prayers, gifts, pictures and messages into the back of an open truck. Once the grass bank was cleared, they mowed it, and left. The only trace of the murder scene was a handful of ribbons and messages still tied to the fence, and the wind and rain soon dealt with them. It was as though nothing but concrete and lawn had ever been there.

That's the thing about the edgelands. They're unmanaged, and that's the secret of their strength. They can survive the rise and fall of many a human project. Redbrick walls from long-abandoned industries crumble next to brand new metal depots and glass office blocks. Eventually, all these buildings will cave in too, because the wilderness cannot be tamed for long.

One day, tourists will come to look at this place to feed their spirits, to take a break from town or countryside. They'll bring picnics, cameras, sketch books. All beauty is learnt. Mountains were seen as ugly and evil a couple of centuries back. Sooner or later, people will stop driving through here with their minds closed. One day, they'll wake up to the edgelands.

TJ and I stick to our agreement to consult on the location for the end of the alphabet. It is just too important and besides, it's nearly done. It makes sense to both of us to map it out away from the flats, on neutral ground. So we fix to meet in the Huntsman bar one lunchtime, when it should be quiet.

And so it is. When I get there, the place is empty except for a barman reading a newspaper, and TJ standing at a fruit machine, pushing buttons. He still insists on wearing white. TJ is all or nothing. He's in a dark pub with tobacco-coloured walls, cigarette in one hand, the other trying to line up three straight bells or lemons. His pint is resting on top of the machine which rocks every time he hits a button. He's wearing white trainers, a white track suit – picked up from a charity shop – and a dirty white T-shirt under it. I buy myself a drink and we sit down at a corner table.

'Where this time, boss?' TJ likes to play the side-kick. It annoyed me at first, but I've learnt to go along with it. He tells me we need to act fast. He says we have to finish it within the next few days, or all that work will be in vain. He says he's sure the police will be back soon, and I don't disagree.

'It's the big one. We need to think carefully.' I start to talk about the Z, the importance of choosing the right location to finish, but he's not listening. He's looking around at the empty bar.

'What is it, TJ?'

'The last time I was in here, there was a hack sniffing around, asking if Michelle was pregnant.'

'No one knew that.'

'You'd be surprised. There was a lot of talk.'

We are keeping our voices almost to whispers. The bar is quiet and the barman keeps glancing up from his newspaper.

'What sort of talk?'

'You didn't hear it then?'

Two old men walk in together. One of them looks over at us and nods, then they start talking to the barman. He folds his newspaper and begins to pour their drinks. We feel able to talk a little louder.

'TJ, stop winding me up.'

'I'm not. It's just I still find it hard to talk about.' He zips up his jacket, as if he's suddenly felt a chill. I'm reminded of the weight he carries in his pockets. He picks up a beer mat and starts tearing strips off it as he speaks.

'I was Jake's mate.'

'Sure, I know.'

'But he could be a bastard.'

'Right.'

The old men break into a laugh about something. The barman puts two pints of Guinness on the bar, and one of the men starts drawing with his finger in the cream at the top. TJ is struggling to say what he has to say, but I'm not going to interrupt him.

'Michelle was a good-looking girl.' I nod. 'Well, Jake talked her into giving Sligo the come-on, to make him think his luck was in, then make a jerk of him. Jake liked to wind Sligo up.'

TJ pauses as one of the old men looks across to us. He lowers his voice and carries on in whispers.

'But it didn't work out. Michelle gave Sligo the come-on, but she must have liked him, or felt sorry for him.'

The old man walks over, and puts his pint of Guinness down on the table between us.

'You be the judges, lads. Is that a fine shamrock, or is that a fine shamrock?'

His friend is heckling from the bar, and the barman is shouting that shamrocks should be made with the tap, not the finger. TJ says he doesn't know what a shamrock should look like and gets up to pump the fruit machine again. I stay and give my verdict, and I have to say it is a fine shamrock, even if it was done with an old man's finger.

I'm looking for signs now, for signs and wonders, as the alphabet gets closer to completion.

This may have been nothing, but I took it as a sign. A couple of nights ago, out on the streets with Paddy, we noticed something in the air. I say 'we', because he stopped in mid-stride and sniffed around him, just as I stopped and held out my hands. It was like an invisible, icy rain, weightless but electric. It felt as though it should have made a sound, a high-pitched sound like chime bars, but it was completely silent. It lasted long enough for us to pause and try to place it, then it stopped.

We turned into the park and the dog ran off as usual. I found him by the maned wolf's cage. Paddy was flat to the floor, calm but alert, watching. I shone the torch and caught the wolf's bright brown eyes. I held them in the beam for a second, then they dipped, and she buried her nose in a hunk of fresh meat. We stayed and watched her finish the meal, licking the traces of blood from round her mouth. Then she sloped into the shelter at the back of her cage, and vanished.

XXVI

I've always admired the chutzpah of it – a rare picture of the master on a job. He must have trusted someone with his camera, because it isn't hanging round his neck. *Weegee and a Body in a Trunk* is the title in the books, but the title undersells it. It's night-time as always, on a piece of New York waste ground, with man-high weeds across the background. In the right foreground is a trunk with the lid open. In the left foreground is Mr Arthur Fellig in his shabby suit, hat, striped tie.

The high angle of the shot shows the crammed, folded body of a man in a pinstriped suit. They've taken his shoes off – presumably to help with the fit – and his arm is twisted back on itself, possibly broken. It's the presence of ropes that makes it look like a trick. There's a coiled rope on the ground next to the trunk, and a thinner rope around his wrist and ankle. He looks like an escapologist, a man attempting the ultimate escape from death itself.

The best bit is Mr Fellig. He's leaning over the trunk, with his lips pursed in speech, as if he's encouraging the escapologist to break that one last rope. Maybe he's giving him instructions, telling him the magic word. I like to think it could be called *Weegee Raises the Dead*.

Of all the murder scenes, why did he choose to be pictured at this one? Well, he was getting a lick of fame on his tongue by then, and he liked the taste. That picture was sheer chutzpah.

Perry and a Body in a Warehouse doesn't cut much as a title either, but it's much the same sort of shot. I'm pulling it out of the tray and I'm pleased with the symmetry. One thing's for sure; this is going to be another Untaken Photograph.

I'm in the left of frame, leaning over like Weegee, lips pursed. On the floor in the right of frame, hunched against the back wall, is the corpse of Adam Sligo. The real and original Adam Sligo. Dead for a while, I'd say. He's dressed in blue and white ski gear, the last outfit he stole from the Bluebird Centre. He's surrounded by wrappers and remnants from weeks of living wild. On the damp grey wall behind him, as neatly as I could manage on the rough stone, is a big scarlet Z. I had considered painting it directly onto him – on his skin or clothes. After all, he needed redemption more than most. But there was too much red around anyway. The bullet he'd used to end his own story had made a real mess of him.

I felt sorry for the man, but there was nothing I could do except give him the Z. Sooner or later, some kids will come across him and call the police. Until then, I want him to spend some time with the alphabet. He didn't paint a single letter of it – despite the rumours – but now he will at least get to feel its power.

It was worth marking with a picture. Some might think we just got lucky, out in the edgelands hunting down locations for the Z, when we found the most perfect location of them all in a boarded-up warehouse. Was it just chance that we were able to bless Sligo with the last letter? I think not. I like to think it's the alphabet beginning to work. We are so close to the end that some of its power is seeping through. What I'm saying is, the alphabet is helping us to finish it.

Of course, I got some good shots of the Z on its own, but when I saw the potential for a Weegee pastiche, it was too good to miss. I gave the camera to TJ and stood in shot.

Yes, it was chutzpah, but not only that. It was a tribute to Fellig, the master.

I've started watching the Sligo video again. I'll have obsessive phases with it, where I'll watch every night, rewind and play, rewind and play. The first time I saw it, I came out admiring him – his deft shoplifting, his smart disguises. This time, I've got nothing but pity for him.

TJ didn't tell me much about Sligo and Michelle, but enough to make me wind back the scene in the toyshop over and over. He walks in, among shelves of wooden toys and racks of baby clothes, and seems to crumble. On the outside, he looks like a shopper who's blundered into the wrong store. But it's all in his eyes, the only time he ever looks up at the camera. All the despair, loss, grief is there. I pause it, and it shivers. He quakes as he stares at me. To my astonishment, I find I'm crying for him. On a single night, in a single moment, he became a murderer, a jilted lover, perhaps a grieving father.

His hideout at the Bluebird, his plastic Aztec temple, must be a twist of black gum now. The fake jungle round it will be wasteland. To Adam on the tape, as he slips between the trees, it must have seemed like Eden. In the heart of the garden, he had made a home for himself and his pregnant Eve, with a selection of stolen clothes and a pair of camping stools facing each other. But Eve wasn't coming. He'd made sure of that.

At first, I expected something sudden and dramatic. The Z was painted, so the act of reclamation was complete. So much had been risked, paid, staked on this.

There were flickers of hope. A group of travellers made camp alongside the nameless lake in the edge-lands, gave it a name *Quickthorn Lake* – and put a sign up. There were no more murders in the town. Once Sligo's body was identified, kids came out to play, and the parks grew busy again.

But the dead were still dead, the grieving still grieved, the lonely still longed. I had expected a real difference, a tangible measure of change. Then I began to worry that we hadn't finished after all. It wasn't working, because we'd missed one letter out.

The O was painted like a barrier round the murder scene. The Q was branded on my poor old lodger's forehead in his sleep. But the P was never found. I'd assumed it had been painted, since the alphabet continued, but now I've changed my mind. Maybe